BIG BAD MAMA

Marjorie Mackenzie leveled the Sharps rifle at Fargo and Gheller—and she looked mighty handy with it.

"I have half a mind to blow you away right here."

"Now, hold on there, old lady," Gheller said. "I haven't done anything wrong."

"I told you to leave my girl be. But this mornin' some of your jackals spotted her and gave chase—"

"Only to ask if you two would join me for supper," Gheller broke in. "You know how I feel about your daughter. Do you really think I'd harm her?"

The mother stepped forward, now looking at Fargo. "Who're you? One of this galoot's gunnies?"

"No," Fargo said. He felt no need to elaborate.

Marjorie's eye narrowed. "You're a liar. Beth told me about a fella she ran into today, and you fit the bill." She swung the Sharps toward him. "I hate liars. Maybe I should put a bullet into you so Gheller her-e'll take the hint." She thumbed back the hammer and aimed dead between Fargo's eyes. "Any last words?"

THE

TRAILSMAN

#237

DAKOTA DAMNATION

by

Jon Sharpe

A SIGNET BOOK

SIGNET
Published by New American Library, a division of
Penguin Putnam Inc., 375 Hudson Street,
New York, New York 10014, U.S.A.
Penguin Books Ltd, 27 Wrights Lane,
London W8 5TZ, England
Penguin Books Australia Ltd, Ringwood,
Victoria, Australia
Penguin Books Canada Ltd, 10 Alcorn Avenue,
Toronto, Ontario, Canada M4V 3B2
Penguin Books (N.Z.) Ltd, 182–190 Wairau Road,
Auckland 10, New Zealand

Penguin Books Ltd, Registered Offices:
Harmondsworth, Middlesex, England

First published by Signet, an imprint of New American Library,
a division of Penguin Putnam Inc.

First Printing, July 2001
10 9 8 7 6 5 4 3 2

The first chapter of this book originally appeared in *Denver City Gold*,
the two hundred thirty-sixth volume in this series.

 REGISTERED TRADEMARK—MARCA REGISTRADA

Printed in the United States of America

PUBLISHER'S NOTE
This is a work of fiction. Names, characters, places, and incidents either are
the product of the author's imagination or are used fictitiously, and any
resemblance to actual persons, living or dead, business establishments, events,
or locales is entirely coincidental.

The Trailsman

Beginnings . . . they bend the tree and they mark the man. Skye Fargo was born when he was eighteen. Terror was his midwife, vengeance his first cry. Killing spawned Skye Fargo, ruthless, cold-blooded murder. Out of the acrid smoke of gunpowder still hanging in the air, he rose, cried out a promise never forgotten.

The Trailsman they began to call him all across the West: searcher, scout, hunter, the man who could see where others only looked, his skills for hire but not his soul, the man who lived each day to the fullest, yet trailed each tomorrow. Skye Fargo, the Trailsman, the seeker who could take the wildness of a land and the wanting of a woman and make them his own.

The Dakota Territory, 1861 —
Where the pursuit of gold drives men to ruin,
and honor among thieves is unknown.

1

The big man in buckskins rode alertly, his right hand resting on the smooth butt of the Colt nestled on his right hip. His piercing lake-blue eyes constantly roved the rugged terrain seeking movement. His ears, like those of his splendid pinto stallion, were pricked to catch the slightest sounds. They were winding up a narrow valley sliced by a gurgling stream, along a rutted excuse for a road that bordered the waterway. Stands of oak, cottonwoods, and ash trees towered on either side. Wildflowers sprinkled the adjacent slopes between ranks of spruce and junipers. Songbirds warbled merrily, and in a meadow to the west mule deer grazed contentedly.

A peaceful enough scene, but Skye Fargo wasn't fooled. The newly created Dakota Territory was a hotbed of violence and bloodshed. Outlaws roamed at will with little fear of being brought to bay, not when lawmen were so few and so very far between. Grizzlies marauded in large numbers. But the greatest threat, by far, was posed by the Sioux, who claimed much of the Dakota Territory as their own and keenly resented white intrusions. Lone travelers like him were easy pickings for roving bands of young warriors eager to count coup and make a name for themselves.

In the past six months alone over a dozen known deaths had been reported. That didn't take into account another seven people who went missing with no clue to their fate. As an old-timer had commented to Fargo shortly before he left Kansas City for the frontier, "The Dakota Territory ain't no place for greenhorns."

Only a few settlements had sprung up and they were well to the southeast. Fargo had passed them days ago. So when he came across a road where there shouldn't have been one, he decided it was worth investigating.

The sun was at its zenith. Fargo had been in the saddle since dawn and needed to stretch his legs. The Ovaro could also use a breather. A grassy clearing seemed the ideal spot. As he reined up in the center and dismounted, a squirrel scolded him from a nearby oak.

Fargo led the stallion to the stream so it could slake its thirst. Removing his hat, he slapped dust from his buckskins, then sank onto a knee and dipped his right hand in the swiftly flowing water. Cupping some, he took a few sips, savoring the cool, refreshing taste, and was about to splash some on his forehead and neck when the stallion twisted its neck to look behind them and whinnied.

In one motion Fargo spun and dropped his wet hand toward the holstered Colt, but he was still too slow. A slender figure at the edge of the trees was already holding a rifle on him, cocked and tucked to one shoulder.

"Don't even think it, mister. I'll scatter your brains from here to Sunday."

Fargo didn't know which surprised him more, that he had been caught off guard, or that the figure, who wore a floppy hat and baggy homespun clothes, was a woman. He couldn't see much of her face but there was no mistaking her gender. Lustrous raven curls spilled from under the hat, and the loose folds of her shirt did little to hide her more-than-ample bosom. "There's no need for the gun," he said quietly.

"I'll be the judge of that." She warily advanced, the rifle rock-steady. Fargo guessed she was in her early to middle twenties. She had full red lips perpetually formed into a delightful pucker, an oval chin, and high cheekbones. "Hike your hands and be quick about it."

Smiling, Fargo complied. "Do you live around here?"

The young woman stopped and studied him from under her hat brim. Intense green eyes raked him from head to foot. "Aubrick or Lodestone, which?"

"How's that?" Fargo responded, unsure of what she meant.

"Are your ears plugged with wax? Are you an Aubrick man or a Lodestone man?"

"Lady, I'm just passing through. I don't have any idea what you're talking about." Fargo didn't like staring down the muzzle of her Spencer. He considered jumping her and decided against it. One twitch of her finger and the rifle would go off.

The woman glanced at the sweaty Ovaro. "So you say. But you could be lyin'. Not that it matters all that much. Ma and me are well shed of the whole rotten business. It cost us too much." Her voice was a low, throaty purr. Combined with her natural beauty, it lent her a sensual allure most any male would find captivating.

Fargo wriggled his fingers. "How about letting me lower my arms? I promise to behave myself."

"You expect me to trust a total stranger?" She chuckled. "You must take me for a yack. Keep your hands right where they are. I'll be out of your hair right quick. I thought you might be one of Benedict's men—" She stopped and tilted her head, listening.

Fargo heard it, too. The drum of hoofs approaching along the road from the north. Suddenly the young woman pivoted and bolted, flying into the vegetation like a frightened doe fleeing from a pack of wolves. Not knowing what to make of her antics, Fargo dropped his hands to his sides at the very moment four riders galloped into view, riding hellbent for leather. At the sight of him they slowed and veered toward the clearing.

Fargo took an instant dislike to the quartet. All four bore the unmistakable stamp of hardcases: cold, cruel expressions, revolvers tied low, and a predatory air, like four hawks swooping in for a kill. They drew rein five yards away, fanning out as they stopped.

"Who the hell are you, mister?" demanded the tallest. For his height he had a pudgy build, with considerably more stomach than chest. A Remington was strapped to his left hip, butt-forward for a cross draw. The rest of him wore cheap store-bought clothes, a faded cowhide vest, and scuffed boots.

"Someone who doesn't like being asked questions," Fargo replied harshly.

"Isn't that a shame," said a small bundle of muscle in a fairly new short-brimmed black hat, black jacket and pants, and a black leather gun belt studded with silver stars. He had blond hair and icy gray eyes. "We mean to ask you some whether you like it or not." Sitting straighter in the saddle, he declared, "I'm Benedict. Cass Benedict."

The name was familiar. Fargo had heard it somewhere or other in his wide-flung travels, but he couldn't say exactly where.

Benedict propped both hands on his saddle horn and leaned forward. "Aubrick or Lodestone?"

There it was again. The same strange question the woman had asked. Fargo didn't answer, and after a bit the rider on the right, a stocky gent who favored a Smith and Wesson, placed his hand on it.

"Cougar got your tongue, mister?" asked the third, teasing the butt of his Smith and Wesson while he spoke. "We don't take kindly to folks who put on airs."

"And I don't take kindly to jackasses who think they can push others around," Fargo responded. He kept a steady eye on the man's gun hand, and when it wrapped around the Smith and Wesson and started to rise, he drew his Colt in a blur, thumbing back the hammer as he leveled it. In a heartbeat the stocky gunman transformed to stone with his Smith and Wesson only halfway out of its holster. "Jerk that iron and it'll be the last mistake you ever make," Fargo vowed.

The fourth rider, a kid no older than sixteen, whooped and slapped a thigh. "Whooee! Did you see that feller slap leather? I only ever saw one person as fast! He's greased lightning, Cass, just like you."

"Shut up, Kenny," Cass Benedict said, and the kid promptly did. Benedict's gray eyes narrowed with renewed interest as he studied Fargo exactly as the young

4

woman had done minutes earlier. "You have a name, friend?"

Fargo nodded.

"But you're not going to tell me, is that how it is?" Smiling thinly, Benedict gazed at the hardcase with the Smith and Wesson. "Unless you're hankering to become worm food, Mort, take your damn hand off that hogleg. Do it nice and slow or I'll shoot you my own self for letting him get the drop on you."

Mort reluctantly unwrapped his fingers and elevated his arm. "He took me by surprise, Cass. I can beat most anyone. You know that."

"Most anyone," Benedict repeated, with a meaningful look at Fargo. "All right, mister. We'll be on our way. Just answer me one thing. Did you happen to see a girl go traipsing by? A cute filly with long curly hair?"

"Do you see a girl here anywhere?" Fargo retorted, and wagged the Colt. "Light a shuck before I lose my temper."

Benedict lifted his reins. "I never argue with an hombre who's holding a six-shooter on me. But you'd better hope we don't run into each other again. Next time things will be a heap different." Breaking into a trot, he led his three companions southward, and as they went around the bend Mort shifted and bestowed a withering glare.

As the hammering hoofs faded, Fargo twirled the Colt into its holster and turned in the direction the young woman had gone. He glimpsed her a hundred yards off, on the other side of the stream, running lithely up a slope, her hat off, her long hair streaming. She had cleverly doubled back and was now safe from Benedict's bunch. As he watched, she came to the tree line and paused to look over her shoulder. Was it his imagination, or did she smile before vanishing into the pines?

Curious as to where the four gunmen came from, Fargo cut his rest short and forked leather. He continued northward and within a few minutes came to a split in the road at a point where the valley broadened. A tall sign had been erected. Near the top was a poorly carved arrow pointing to the northeast. Scribbled on it was the word AUBRICK. Underneath was a second arrow pointing to the northwest, with the word LODESTONE.

Fargo had his explanation. Aubrick and Lodestone were settlements or towns, most likely. But he couldn't understand why the young woman and Cass Benedict had been so interested in which one he came from.

Clucking to the pinto, Fargo headed toward Aubrick. One place was as good as the other so far as he was concerned, so long as it had a saloon. First, though he'd treat himself to a hot meal. The thought of a thick, juicy steak washed down by half a pot of piping-hot coffee made his mouth water.

The road wound past verdant woodland broken by long tracts of prime grazing land. Fargo saw no evidence of cattle though, or any homesteads for that matter. He had gone over half a mile, crossing a stream along the way, when, on rounding a sharp turn, he found himself confronted by three burly men holding shotguns. Beyond them, tethered to a tree, were three horses.

"Hold up there, mister. We want a word with you."

First the young lovely, then Cass Benedict's bunch, and now this. Fargo was in no mood to be imposed upon again and was tempted to apply his spurs to the Ovaro and barrel on past. But none of the trio made a threatening move. To the contrary, the spokesman smiled warmly and came toward the stallion with his rifle cradled in the crook of his elbow and his other hand outstretched to show his intentions were peaceable.

Reining up, Fargo quipped, "If you tell me this is a toll road, I'm turning right around."

The man laughed. He was middle-aged and sported a drooping mustache bushy enough for a bird to build a nest in. "No, nothing like that. We're from Aubrick, is all, and we need to make certain you're not out to cause trouble."

"Why would I want to?" Fargo asked.

"Everyone knows the Lodestone outfit has it in for us," the man said. "Used to be, they'd send men in now and then to stir us up, which was bad enough. But when the raids started, we took to posting guards morning and night."

"Raids?" Fargo repeated, trying to make sense of the information. "Are you telling me the two towns have a feud going?"

"Aubrick and Lodestone are mining camps," the man revealed. "I reckon you're new to these parts or you'd know all about it."

Fargo wanted to question them more, but just then a fourth person arrived on the scene, an attractive woman riding sidesaddle astride a sorrel. Auburn hair framed her lively hazel eyes and pert cheeks, and a prim beige dress clung to her buxom figure. As she came to a stop the three guards turned and squared their shoulders as if they were soldiers on parade.

"Miss Nicholson!" the first man declared. "You shouldn't ought to be out here by your lonesome. It's not safe."

"Oh, posh, Harry," the newcomer said. "Gheller wouldn't stoop so low as to harm a female. Besides, my brother and I were over by the stream and he spotted this gentleman coming up the road and thought we should give him a cordial welcome."

"The parson sent you? Well then, he knows what's best." The three guards stepped to one side to permit the Ovaro to go by. "You heard Miss Nicholson, mister. You're free to do as you please."

Fargo rode on. Up ahead the trees thinned and he could see a few buildings and tents and people moving about. Miss Nicholson brought her sorrel around alongside the stallion, keeping pace. As was apparently the local custom, she scrutinized him closely.

"My, you're a big one. Rather handsome, too, in a roughhewn sort of way." She flashed white, even teeth. "I'm Amanda Nicholson. Please forgive my forwardness. My brother always says I'm too frank for my own good." Amanda showed more pearly teeth. "Arthur is the parson here."

"That's nice," Fargo said to be polite. He was still

thinking of that steak, and later, an evening of cards and liquor. A fallen dove would make the night complete.

"He's in charge, you might say," Amanda prattled on. "It was Arthur who organized the community into standing up to Slan Gheller and those awful gun sharks who do Gheller's dirty work."

"Would Cass Benedict be one of them?" Fargo asked.

Suspicion flared in Amanda's hazel eyes. "You know him, do you? As vile a human being as ever was born, if you want my opinion. He lives by the gun and he'll die by the gun. Folks say he has fourteen kills to his credit, three in Denver last year alone."

The mention jarred Fargo's recollection. Now he knew where he had heard of Benedict before. Last summer there had been a widely reported gunfight in broad daylight on the streets of downtown Denver. Newspaper accounts had it that Benedict, a gambler by trade, had fallen afoul of a local tough by the name of Tantlinger. One thing led to another, and one afternoon Tantlinger and two pards stalked up to Benedict and demanded he leave the Mile High City for healthier climes. Benedict told them to go to hell, and Tantlinger and his men went for their hardware. Cass Benedict shot all three dead. Self-defense, a judge ruled, but the town marshal and a bevy of deputies saw fit to escort Benedict to the city limits and advised him to ply his trade elsewhere. And now here Benedict was, involved in another dispute in a remote valley deep in Dakota Territory.

"He's always so civil and courteous around me," Amanda Nicholson was saying, "but he doesn't fool me for a second. His kind only have one thing on their minds. They're lechers, born and bred."

Fargo glanced at her, and damned if she wasn't serious. "I've never heard tell he mistreats women."

Amanda's chin jutted indignantly. "Have you no sense of decency? How can you defend an animal like him? Men of his ilk only have to look at a woman for her to know what they're thinking."

"Is that a fact?" Fargo imagined how she would look

8

without her prim dress, her auburn tresses spilling over her naked shoulders, and inwardly grinned.

"Absolutely," Amanda declared. "A woman always knows. Our intuition is more finely developed. Out of necessity, I'd warrant. Were it up to you men, there wouldn't be a virgin over fourteen."

"And you're a parson's sister, you say?" Fargo said, impressed with her forthright manner.

To her credit Amanda laughed. "I told you I was too honest for my own good. I don't beat around the bush, sir. I tell things as they are." She paused. "It just dawned on me. I've introduced myself, but you haven't exercised the common courtesy of doing likewise."

Fargo obliged her, adding, "I ran into Benedict back down the road. He was searching for a young woman with black hair and a Spencer."

"That would be Bethany Mackenzie," Amanda said, shaking her head in disapproval. "The wild woman of the hills, she's called hereabouts. Beth and her mother, Marjorie, have a cabin up yonder." Amanda pointed at the hills to the northeast. "They were here long before anyone else. Her father, Finnian, was a prospector."

"Was?"

"Fin was found dead about four months ago, shortly after Aubrick was founded. Ironic, when you think about it, since he was the one who first discovered gold. If not for him, none of the rest of us would be here."

Fargo almost reined up in surprise. "There's been a strike?" Ordinarily, word of new gold finds spread like prairie fire. The latest, in the Rockies, started a gold rush that was still underway, with people streaming in from all over creation.

"That there has," Amanda confirmed, "and we're doing our utmost to keep the news hushed up. The people here don't want droves of claim jumpers moving in on digs that are rightfully theirs." She stared toward the north end of the valley, where chalky cliffs and rocky gorges replaced the greenery. "And, too, most of the finds so far have been small. But there's hope that any day now someone will hit the mother lode, and before you can say John Jacob Astor, we'll have more money than we know what to do with.''

Astor, as Fargo recalled, had at one time been the richest man in America. "So how did you and everyone else hear about the gold?''

"Fin made a mistake," Amanda said. "He needed supplies. So he packed up his wife and daughter and went to Fort Randall.''

Fargo had visited the post numerous times. It was situated on a plateau about a quarter of a mile from the Missouri River, and had been built to help keep the Sioux and Poncas in line.

Amanda went on. "While there he drank a bit too much and let slip to a buffalo hunter he knew that he'd found some color. He made the fellow promise not to tell anyone, but the hunter told a friend who told another friend who told—" She stopped, and chortled. "Well, you get the notion. Before long over fifty people were up here.''

"That's how many live in Aubrick?''

"No. About half that now," Amanda said. "The rest moved across the stream when Gheller set up his own mining camp, Lodestone." She extended a finger.

Fargo looked, and on the other side of the stream, approximately two hundred yards distant, was another collection of tents and several ramshackle buildings. "Why did they start their own camp?" It was smarter for everyone to stick together, what with the Sioux on the prod.

Amanda scowled in the general direction of Lodestone. "Blame Gheller. He sent for a pack of gun sharks, and the next thing we knew, he unleashed every debauchery known to man. So my brother ran him out.''

They rounded the last bend. A dozen dilapidated tents and a few crudely constructed buildings were scattered at random like warts on a toad's back, awash in the stark glare of the afternoon sun. Two of the buildings were log affairs, another a rickety plank building that bore in bold red letters a sign proclaiming it was THE HOLY TABERNACLE OF THE MOST HIGH GOD.

Nowhere, Fargo noticed, was there a saloon.

"My brother came up with the name," Amanda said, nodding at the church. "Quite ear-catching, don't you think?"

"Where can a man get a drink around here?" Fargo asked, drawing rein.

"A drink? You mean hard liquor?" Amanda sniffed as if she smelled a rank odor. "Mr. Fargo, Aubrick isn't like all those mining camps in the Rockies. We don't let Satan run amok." She gazed past him, and brightened. "Here. I'll let Arthur explain. He's the one keeping the tide of darkness at bay."

A sandy-haired man in a black frock coat and starched white shirt had emerged from the church and was strolling toward them, a leather-bound Bible clutched to his chest. He had bony features, long limbs, and a broomstick body. He smiled when he saw them, but the smile didn't touch his dark eyes. "Amanda! Is this the rider your brother spotted?"

"His name is Fargo. A frontiersman, on his way across the territory. I've invited him to partake of our hospitality."

Arthur Nicholson, at your service, Brother Fargo," the pastor said, offering a skinny hand. "We cordially welcome you to our humble haven. You have merely to ask and we still strive to fill your every need."

"He wants a drink," Amanda said distastefully. "The hundred-proof variety."

Arthur clucked like a hen chastising one of its brood. "I'm afraid you won't find any demon rum or other liquid abominations in Aubrick. We believe in living decent, upright lives. All earthly vices are forbidden."

"*All* of them?" Fargo asked. So much for spending the night with a willing dove.

"All those the Good Book prohibits, yes." Arthur affectionately patted his Bible and recited a litany of banned behaviors. "No gambling, no drinking, no loose women, no swearing, no spitting. Thou shalt not kill. Thou shalt not steal. Thou shalt not commit adultery. Thou shalt not covet thy neighbor's house. Thou shalt

11

not covet thy neighbor's wife, nor his male servant, nor his female servant, nor his ox, nor his donkey, nor anything that is your neighbor's.''

"Is that all?" Fargo asked dryly.

"Oh, mercy, no," Arthur said. "I have a list posted in the tabernacle of all four hundred and twenty-seven temptations we must shun."

"Four hundred?" Fargo wasn't a Bible-thumper, but he'd known a few men of the cloth, decent, honorable men who had devoted their lives to the uplifting of human souls, and he couldn't recall any of them ever mentioning *that* many vices.

"We live according to Scripture," Arthur declared. "And by every prohibition in every book in both the Old and the New Testaments." Quickly opening his Bible, he flipped through the pages until he found the passage he sought. "He that smiteth a man, so that he die, shall surely be put to death. And he that curseth his father, or his mother, shall surely be put to death—"

'For swearing?" Fargo said in disbelief.

Arthur Nicholson hadn't appeared to hear. "Eye for eye, tooth for tooth, hand for hand, foot for foot. Burning for burning, wound for wound, stripe for stripe." He snapped the book shut. " 'The heavens declare the glory of God, and the firmament showeth His handiwork.' "

All this time people had been converging. The majority were men, shabbily dressed, dirty and haggard, their hostility thick enough to cut with a blunt knife. Several saw fit to surround the stallion, including a brawny slab of sinew in dirty overalls, a pick slanted across his wide shoulder. "Who's this, then, Parson?" the slab demanded of Arthur. "Another of Gheller's curly wolves?"

Amanda answered him. "He has nothing to do with Gheller, Lon Wolgast. So I'll thank you to treat him with more courtesy than you did our last visitor."

Wolgast had eyes a ferret would envy and a square jaw sprinkled with grizzle. "I only have our best interests at heart, Miss Nicholson. You and your brother never think ill of anyone. But this feller sure has the stamp of a gunman, if you ask me."

"That he does," another man agreed.

Wolgast stepped closer to the Ovaro. "What's your handle, mister? And tell the truth. If I suspect you're lying, we'll go through your saddlebags for proof."

Fargo's temper flared. He had been imposed on one too many times, and there were limits to how much he would abide. "No one lays a hand on my saddlebags but me."

"Is that so?" Wolgast sneered, and reached up.

"Lon, don't!" Amanda scolded. "I brought him here, and I won't have you bullying him. If you must know, he told me his name is Fargo—"

"Fargo?" Wolgast said in mild alarm. "I've heard that name before. I can't rightly remember when, but I'm sure it had something to do with a gunfight." His sneer returned. "So you're a gun fanner, mister. And that means Slan Gheller sent for you. Which makes you our enemy."

Arthur Nicholson raised a hand. "Brother Wolgast, please. We shouldn't jump to conclusions."

"Speak for yourself, Parson," Wolgast growled. "I've put up with all of Gheller's shenanigans I'm going to take. It's about time we learned him a lesson." And with that, Wolgast lunged, grabbed Fargo by the front of his buckskin shirt, and hauled him from the saddle.

—

2

West of the muddy Mississippi there were certain things a man never did. Foremost was stealing another's horse. Stranding someone afoot was tantamount to condemning them to death, which was why horse thieves were summarily hanged. Similarly, a man had to ensure he was never caught cheating at cards. Cheating itself was common, but getting caught wasn't tolerated and invariably led to the cheater doing a strangulation jig at a hemp social. The third taboo was much more basic. Under no circumstances whatsoever should a man put his hands on another. It just wasn't done. In a land where eight out of ten men went around heeled, anyone who overstepped his bounds invited swift and lethal retaliation.

Skye Fargo hadn't figured Lon Wolgast would be foolhardy enough to assault him. Not when he was wearing a Colt and all Wolgast had was a pick. He had to remind himself that some people had more space between their ears than there was on the prairie, especially toughs like Wolgast who thought their size and bulk gave them the right to go around doing as they damned well pleased.

Fargo intended to teach him differently.

As Wolgast yanked him off the Ovaro, Fargo twisted, balled his fist, and slammed it against the hothead's jaw. Wolgast staggered back, losing his grip, and shook his head to clear it.

"Here, now!" Arthur Nicholson called out. "We'll have none of that! Violence is forbidden."

Wolgast didn't care. He hiked the pick to swing, and

Fargo waded in. A right cross rocked Wolgast on his boot heels. A left uppercut sent him tottering onto his backside in the dirt, the heavy pick thudding to the ground beside him.

"Didn't you hear me?" the parson hollered. "We live by the Golden Rule here. I want you to stop this instant."

Snarling like a wild beast, Wolgast gripped his pick and rose. Blood trickled from a corner of his mouth. "I'm going to rip you wide for that, mister. Tear a hole in you from your gut to your spine."

"Brother Wolgast!" Arthur tried one last time. "This man is our guest. Remember the story of the Good Samaritan."

"Remind me sometime, Parson," Wolgast rasped, and sprang, swinging the pick with all his might, in a blow that would fell a bear in its tracks.

Fargo threw himself to the right. The tapered end of the pick flashed past his stomach, missing by the width of a cat's whiskers. He tried to dart nearer, but Wolgast skipped to the rear and swung again. This time the metal tip sheared toward Fargo's face. Barely in time, Fargo jerked back. A puff of air fanned his cheek as the pick cleaved the space his head had occupied a heartbeat ago.

"Stop that, Lon!" Amanda bawled.

Wolgast wasn't to be denied. He swung again and again, the pick always in motion, seeking to prevail by sheer force. Spite animated his features, spite that worsened when Fargo sidestepped an overhand arc and connected with a couple of quicksilver jabs. Jarred, but far from beaten, Wolgast firmed his grip on the pick's long handle, roared like a grizzly, and whipped the pick on high.

Levering on his boot heels, Fargo flung himself into a dive. His right shoulder rammed into Wolgast's legs and they both went down, Wolgast on the bottom. Fargo seized the pick handle in his left hand to prevent it from being swung, while simultaneously raining a series of rights to the chin. At the third blow Wolgast abruptly went limp and his hold loosened.

Wrenching the pick loose, Fargo hurled it aside and slowly rose. "Anyone else?" he challenged the onlookers, but none were particularly eager to take up where Wolgast had left off.

Amanda was astounded. "My goodness! I didn't think anyone could beat Lon with their bare hands. He's the strongest man in Aubrick."

"And the most hardheaded," her brother said sadly. "He should have listened to me. The Good Book admonishes us to love our brethren, not impale them on picks. The Lord has seen fit to punish him for his arrogance."

"I think his nose is busted," someone commented.

Arthur came over and placed a hand on Fargo's arm. "I pray you will find it in your heart to forgive him, Brother."

"Like hell," Fargo muttered. Taking hold of the Ovaro's reins, he scanned the camp. "Since I can't get a drink around here, is there someplace I can get something to eat?"

Amanda stepped around Wolgast's unconscious form. "I'm afraid we don't have a restaurant as yet. That will come when more people arrive. But Arthur and I would love to have you for supper." She smiled self-consciously. "I'm a good cook, if I do say so myself."

"That she is," Parson Nicholson confirmed. "We eat promptly at five, and we'd be delighted to have you share our bounty."

Fargo hesitated. They meant well, but he had a hunch they would serve up more than food and he wasn't partial to having his ears bent for hours on end about the glories of the hereafter. Not that he looked down his nose at religious sorts, as some did. He just didn't like it when others tried to shove their beliefs down his throat. "I wouldn't want to impose," he said to justify refusing.

"Nonsense!" the parson exclaimed. "Everyone is welcome at our table, sinners and saved alike." He winked. "I promise not to bore you to death by reciting the Psalms from memory."

"Please accept," Amanda urged. "I'll set out our best dishes and treat you to a feast fit for King Solomon."

Against his better judgment, Fargo nodded.

"Excellent!" Arthur said. He turned to Wolgast, who was beginning to groan. "Now then, would several of you fine fellows be so kind as to carry our errant brother over to his tent? I need to have a talk with him. Apparently my preaching has failed to take root and I must remedy my oversight."

Fargo squinted up at the sun. It was about half past one, which meant he had three and a half hours to kill until supper. He decided to see what Aubrick had to offer, if anything. As he trudged on between two tents, Amanda Nicholson fell into step beside him. "Shouldn't you be cutting up potatoes or something?"

"There's plenty of time for that, Brother Fargo," she said with a smile.

Fargo looked her up and down, deliberately lingering at the swell of her cleavage. "Let's get one thing straight, lady. I'm not your brother and I never will be. I've been on the trail for days, and I could use a bath, a stiff drink, some hot food, and a woman whose scruples aren't as rigid as yours." He assumed she would be offended and traipse off in a huff, but once again she surprised him.

"A bath, you say? Then this is your lucky day. My brother and I happen to have the only washtub in the whole camp. Everyone else bathes in the stream." Amanda crooked a finger. "Follow me, Bro—" she caught herself and grinned. "Follow me, sir. I can have enough water heated up in about fifteen minutes."

There was no hitch rail in front of the church so Fargo looped the stallion's reins around a nail jutting from the wall, shucked his Henry from the saddle scabbard, and entered on Amanda's heels.

The Holy Tabernacle Of The Most High God looked as if it had been thrown together in a single afternoon by half a dozen drunks. Some of the vertical planks were half an inch apart, others leaned slightly to either side, and the roof had a large hole in it. "Where they ran out of planks," Amanda explained. Narrōw benches served

17

as pews, benches cobbled together from uneven pieces of wood, resulting in lopsided seats. The podium, such as it was, consisted of an upended barrel placed on two-by-fours, which in turn rested on large flat rocks. Beyond was a doorway, minus a door.

"These are our living quarters," Amanda grandly announced, as if she were ushering him into the finest suite of the finest hotel in New Orleans.

The only improvement Fargo noticed was that the planks fit more snugly. That, and the furniture had been made by craftsmen who knew what they were doing. A cabinet sat against the far wall, a cupboard hung on another. Near it was a stove that had seen better days and a wood box crammed with broken branches.

"We have four rooms counting this one," Amanda crowed. "My brother and I each have our own bedrooms, and there's a bath." She stepped to a doorway on the right. "It's a little cramped."

Fargo walked over "A little" was an understatement. It wasn't a room, it was a closet, and the only object in it was a waist-high tub pitted with rust. The tub scarcely fit.

"Would you care for some coffee while you're waiting for the water to heat up?" Amanda asked, flitting to the cupboard.

"Why not?" Fargo said. Claiming a chair at the table, he leaned his rifle against the wall.

"So tell me," Amanda said as she opened a can of Arbuckle's, "are you married, perchance? A handsome devil like you must have a wife hid somewhere."

"If I do, I don't know about it," Fargo quipped, pushing his hat back on his head. She giggled and bent over the stove to light it, and he admired how her dress outlined the shapely contours of her thighs.

"My, my. That makes you an eligible bachelor doesn't it?" Amanda regarded him slyly. "Are you in the market for someone to warm your bed at night?"

For a parson's sister, Fargo reflected, she was uncommonly forthright about a subject most women wouldn't discuss in mixed company. "Can't say that I am, no," he truthfully responded.

"Ah. More's the pity. Every man needs a good woman." Amanda paused, then said more to herself than to him, "And every woman needs a good man."

"A pretty woman like you shouldn't have any trouble finding one," Fargo commented.

About to place a log in the stove, Amanda frowned. "Would that it were true. But men tend to shy away from me. I think it's because of my bother. Since he's a pastor, they jump to the conclusion I must be just as pure of spirit as he is. They place me on a pedestal and treat me differently than they do other women. You have no idea how aggravating that is." She added the log, then some kindling, lit it, and puffed lightly until flames crackled. Uncurling, she said wistfully, "I can't remember the last time a man kissed me."

Fargo gazed at her ripe, full lips, twin strawberries waiting to be tasted. "That's a sin," he remarked.

Amanda burst out laughing. "I couldn't have expressed it better myself. If I had any sense, I'd strike out on my own. Go to a big city where no one knows me and have more suitors than I can count."

"Why don't you?"

Amanda sighed. "I can't bring myself to leave Arthur. We're very close, he and I, closer than most brothers and sisters. Our folks died when we were little and we were raised by an aunt who despised us and worked us to death." She filled a coffeepot with water from a bucket on the counter. "Aunt Susan. A harpy if ever there was one. She quoted the Good Book by the hour, but she didn't have a spark of love in her soul."

A transformation came over Amanda. Her lovely features contorted into a mark of fierce hatred, a change so startling that Fargo had the illusion he was staring at another woman.

"She was fond of a hickory switch. Five or six times a day she'd take Arthur or me out to the woodshed and tan our bottoms for what she called 'infractions.' Sometimes she dragged us out there because she suspected us of having impure thoughts, so she'd beat us to banish them." Amanda tittered coldly. "It got so we loathed her as much as she loathed us. But Aunt Susan got her due comeuppance in the end. Yes, indeed."

"What happened?" Fargo prodded when she fell silent.

With a visible effort Amanda composed herself. "Why, it was the darnedest thing. She stepped out into the street without looking and was trampled by a horse and carriage. The wheels crushed her neck. I was only a few feet away and heard it snap." Amanda set the pot on one of the griddles. "Sweetest sound I ever did hear. I only wish I could have snapped it with my own two hands."

Fargo made a mental note to avoid making Amanda angry, and if he did, to never turn his back on her.

She faced him, smiling serenely. "Mercy me, what you must be thinking! That wasn't very nice, was it? Arthur would scold me severely if he overheard." She adopted a contrite look. "I'm afraid I've never been all that good at turning the other cheek and forgiving others their trespasses. I do so hope you won't hold it against me."

"I'm not much for turning the other cheek myself," Fargo admitted.

"Two peas in a pod," Amanda declared, and walked over, her hips swaying enticingly. "I do so hope you're not going to place me on a pedestal like all those other fools. I would be vastly disappointed."

After what Fargo had just witnessed, she had no need to worry. "The only reason I'd ever put a woman on a pedestal would be so I could look up her dress."

Amanda lit up with glee and brazenly stroked his chin. "Something tells me the two of us will get along just dandy."

On an impulse Fargo reached around and cupped her buttocks. She gave a little start, then grinned seductively as he pulled her down toward him. Perching in his lap, she molded her hot mouth to his, her tongue darting between his parted teeth. Hungrily, she sucked on his lips while her hands applied themselves to his shoulders and chest. When at long length she broke for breath, her eyelids were hooded with raw desire.

20

"Oh my. If I wasn't afraid my brother might walk in on us, I'd tear those buckskins off and have my way."

"Don't let that stop you," Fargo teased, lathering her neck and then her ear. She shivered when he sucked on the lobe.

"Keep that up and we'll be the talk of the camp," Amanda said huskily. "They'll hear me scream clear up at the diggings."

"You'd yell for help?" Fargo said, rimming her ear with the tip of his tongue.

"Not that kind of screaming, no." Amanda gasped. "I make a lot of noise when I make love. I know I shouldn't, but I can't help myself." She playfully nipped his cheek with her teeth. "I like it rough and noisy. Aren't I shameless?"

Fargo's answer was to cover both breasts with his hands and squeeze them through the dress. He felt her nipples harden under his palms as she threw back her head and groaned. He was about to fasten his mouth to hers once more when the clomp of shoes warned him they were no longer alone.

Amanda shot to her feet and over to the stove just as her brother was framed in the doorway. She was flushed and breathing heavily, but her back was to him and he didn't seem to notice.

"Is that coffee I smell brewing?" Arthur asked.

"Brother Fargo mentioned he was in need of a bath," Amanda said without turning around. "I offered him the use of our tub, but we'll need more water."

Arthur deposited his Bible on the counter and beckoned to Fargo. "If you'll give me a hand, we'll have you fixed up in no time."

Out back, lined up against the rear of the church, were half a dozen buckets. Four were empty. The parson gave two to Fargo and hoisted the other two himself, saying, "Ordinarily we fill these each evening so we'll have plenty of water the next morning. Follow me." He walked briskly westward along a well-worn footpath that meandered among the tents, smiling at everyone they passed and greeting them with a cheerful, "Good afternoon, Brother!" or "Good afternoon, Sister!"

Aubrick's residents responded in kind. That they thought highly of their spiritual leader was obvious, and it spurred Fargo to comment, "The people here sure like you."

Arthur swelled with pride. "I suppose they see me as their deliverer. Until my sister and I arrived, no one had the gumption to stand up to Slan Gheller. He was free to harvest the fruits of wickedness he so willingly sowed, and as a consequence made life here profoundly miserable."

"What exactly did Gheller do?" Fargo fished for specifics. He assumed it must be a dastardly act along the lines of murder or rape.

"He ran a saloon," Arthur Nicholson said.

Fargo waited for more details and, when none were forthcoming, commented, "You ran him out for *that*?"

"Saloons breed evil, Brother Fargo. They are a step on the road to perdition." The parson grinned at a couple of young children. "You know as well as I do what goes on in them. Gambling, Drinking. Familiarity with loose women."

All of which were some of Fargo's favorite pastimes. "I've been in plenty of towns that had churches and saloons, both."

Arthur shot him a stern glance. "Flocks led by misguided ministers, by men of the cloth who believe it is acceptable to compromise with the forces of darkness. By permitting wickedness to flourish they unwittingly taint their souls and the souls of all those they minister to." He gestured, encompassing all of Aubrick. "It won't happen here. Gambling, liquor, and fornication are abominations unto the Lord and won't be tolerated. Those who practice them will be banished from our community."

"That's what you told Gheller?"

"That, and much more," Arthur said. "I marched into his den of ill repute with my congregation at my back and denounced him for the blackguard and degenerate

22

he is. I commanded him to leave Aubrick or the wrath of the Almighty would descend upon him."

"What did he say?" Fargo couldn't see a saloon owner giving in to such a preposterous demand. Not in a rough-and-tumble mining camp, of all places, as mining camps were notorious havens for vice of every kind.

"What could he say?" the parson rejoined. "I had truth and goodness on my side. He agreed to dismantle his establishment and depart Aubrick within the week. That was two months ago." He gazed across the stream at Lodestone. "I had hoped he would travel a bit farther than he did. So long as he limits his influence to his private domain there is little else I can do."

Something about the whole affair didn't sound quite right, but Fargo dismissed it as none of his business. In a day or so he would be on his way and well shed of their nonsense.

"Every now and then Gheller sends some of his boys over to stir up trouble. Lately, he's taken to having his men harass us at all hours of the day and night. They thunder into Aubrick, whooping and discharging fire-arms, scaring everyone half to death." Arthur passed the last of the tents. "A petty tactic by a peptic man."

"Is he trying to drive your people off?" Fargo asked.

"If so, he's doomed to disappointment. No one has left. In fact, it's firmed their resolve to stick things out." Arthur looked to the north. "Poor, deluded wretches. As if any of them will really strike it rich."

A few hundred feet away lay a barren maze of cliffs, gorges, and gullies. Somewhere in that wasteland the stream had its source—and so did the gold. Two men were in waist-deep, panning industriously. Others were working a sluice. From claims farther away echoed the ring of picks and hammers.

"I've tried to make them understand man can't serve God and Mammon both, but they won't heed," Arthur lamented. "Greed blinds them to their foolishness."

"You haven't staked a claim for yourself?" Fargo asked.

Arthur snorted. "You mock me, brother. I refuse to

succumb to demon wealth. Better to be poor and in God's good graces than rich and fated to writhe in torment in the infernal pits of hell. Were I to be offered a million in gold I would decline out of fear for my eternal welfare."

Fargo wouldn't decline, but he wouldn't let it change him much, either. Buying a fancy mansion and settling down didn't appeal to him, not when there were was so much of the country yet to see, so much yet to do. Maybe he'd buy a saloon, or a whole string, just to have somewhere to rest up from time to time and indulge his passion for poker and the ladies. Not necessarily in that order.

Several matrons in bonnets and long dresses were filling buckets of their own. They were immensely pleased to see the parson and gushed about last Sunday's service and how much they enjoyed his sermon.

Fargo hunkered by the stream and dipped a bucket into a shallow pool. He was unaware another man had come up behind them until the man squatted a few feet away and immersed a canteen.

"Howdy mister." This one wasn't like most of the dirt-poor gold seekers. He wore a new, clean brown suit, a rakish bowler, and shoes that had been polished until they shone. He wasn't wearing a gun belt but a telltale bulge under his jacket hinted at a shoulder rig.

Fargo merely nodded.

"The name is Perry Hutchings. I've only been in Aubrick a week or so. How about you?" Hutchings had beefy features, a sign of too much easy living, and a pale complexion, a sign that until recently he hadn't ventured outdoors a lot.

"My first day," Fargo said. Hutchings's accent pegged him as an Easterner. From Illinois or Indiana, Fargo guessed.

"Good friends of the parson's, I take it? I saw you with Miss Nicholson earlier, and here you are out with the parson himself."

Among Fargo's peeves was a strong dislike for nosy people. He saw no need to respond, and taking the now-full bucket from the stream, he set it beside him and picked up the empty one.

Hutchings glanced at Nicholson, who was in animated conversation with the matrons. "Say, friend," he said quietly so only Fargo heard, "the parson didn't happen to mention where he and his sister are from, did they?"

"No," Fargo said. What that had to do with anything was beyond him.

"Too bad," Hutchings said, and suddenly stiffened when the women headed toward Aubrick and the parson turned.

"Brother Hutchings," Arthur said. "My ears are burning. You weren't just talking about me by any chance, were you?"

"No, sir, Parson," Hutchings said quickly, with an anxious glance at Fargo. Capping the canteen, he rose. "I was making the acquaintance of your friend, here."

"Is that so?" Arthur came to the water's edge. "Sister Williams was telling me how you badgered her with questions about me the other day. And this morning Brother Murphy mentioned you were asking him all sorts of things, too." Arthur's eyes acquired a less-than-brotherly gleam. "Why all this interest in Amanda and me? More to the point, if you have questions, why haven't you come to me?"

"I didn't want to impose." Hutchings slung the canteen over an arm. "I respect you, Parson, and the principles you stand for. I was curious to learn more about you, is all."

"I'll tell you what," Arthur said suavely. "We've invited Brother Fargo for supper. Why don't you join us? I'll be glad to satisfy your curiosity."

The dandy began to back away. "Oh no. I couldn't."

"It wasn't a request, Brother Hutchings," Arthur stated. "I insist you be at the church by five. If you're not, I'll send someone to fetch you."

"In that case I'll be there," Hutchings said without enthusiasm. Rotating on a heel, he swiftly departed.

"What a strange man," the parson said. "I hope I didn't make a mistake inviting him to join our community. We don't need more troublemakers." So saying, he gazed westward, and just as Perry Hutchings had done, he stiffened. "Speaking of troublemakers, here come the worst of the lot."

Fargo saw five men walking toward them from Lodestone, four of whom he recognized; Cass Benedict and his gunnies. With them was a big man in a large white hat. "Who's the one in the middle?" he asked.

"That would be Slan Gheller himself."

3

Skye Fargo was a shrewd judge of men. He had to be in order to survive. The wilderness was home to countless outlaws and renegades, any one of whom would slit his throat without a qualm. Being able to read tracks and animal sign was all well and good, but being able to read men often served him in better stead. For just as he needed to know by a buffalo's stance and bearing whether it was about to charge, so, too, he needed to be able to tell whether the men he met in his travels were harmless or potential threats. Now, as the party from Lodestone drew near, he studied Slan Gheller. Based on what he had heard he expected Lodestone's founder to be a typical sidewinder, arrogant, cold, and vicious. But the man who came to a stop across the stream was anything but.

Smiling broadly, completely at ease, an amused twinkle lighting his dark eyes, Slan Gheller regarded the parson a moment, then said good-naturedly, "You're fetching the water yourself now, Arthur? I thought you always left it up to that feisty sister of yours." Gheller had fleshy, florid features, a bulbous nose, and bushy brows. He looked more like a doting grandfather than the ruthless cutthroat the parson had made him out to be.

"Not always, no." Arthur Nicholson set down his two empty buckets. "What brings you out here, might I ask? It isn't often you tear yourself away from your cards and loose women."

Gheller chortled. "Loose women do wonders to relax

27

a man. You should try one sometime." He turned toward Fargo. "As to why I'm here, Cass spotted your friend, and I thought I'd make his acquaintance. I hear he's mighty slick with that Colt of his."

"Oh?" the parson said.

Fargo straightened, his buckets at his feet, freeing his hands in case the need arose to use them.

Of the four gunmen only Mort seemed inclined to start anything; openly glaring, he held his gun hand above his revolver, his fingers twitching nervously. Kenny, the young one, had his thumbs hooked in his gun belt and was grinning idiotically. Riley looked bored. As for Cass Benedict, he met Fargo's calm gaze with one equally calm, and said, "I told you we'd meet again."

Gheller chopped the air with a fleshy hand. "You're not to start anything, Cass, you hear me? There'll be no blood spilled unless I say so."

Mort's fingers stopped twitching and formed into claws. "That's just it, boss. You never let us throw down on any of these holier-than-thou types. I have a right to kill this one if I want. He made me look stupid earlier."

Fargo sensed what was coming and cleared his head of distracting thoughts.

Gheller tried again. "Making you look stupid isn't hard to do, Mort. You bring it on yourself with that temper of yours. And so long as you work for me you'll do what I say."

"Is that so?" Mort took a step to the right and bent slightly at the waist. "Then how about if I up and quit right here and now? I'm tired of you riding herd on us. I've got something to prove to myself and nothing you can say or do will stop me."

"Don't!" Gheller commanded, but it was no use.

Grinning wolfishly at Fargo, Mort declared, "You won't be so lucky this time, bastard. I'm ready for you. Whenever you want, try for that hogleg. You'll never clear leather."

"One of us won't," Fargo agreed.

Slan Gheller and the others backed away. Seasoned hands at gunplay, they weren't eager to take a stray slug.

"You'd best hope he kills you, Mort," Gheller said. "Because if he doesn't, when I get through with you, you'll wish he had."

The tip of Mort's tongue rimmed his thin lips. He was almost ready. Fargo could see it in his eyes, could see Mort marshaling the courage, see Mort's whole body tense. The gunman was a keg of black powder about to explode. Another second, and in a twinkling Mort's right hand darted to his Smith and Wesson. He was fast, truly fast, and with practiced skill he started to jerk his six-gun, his thumb curling around the hammer so he could pull it back as he drew.

Fargo never gave him the chance. The Colt leaped into his hand and he banged off two shots so swiftly they sounded as one.

Mort was punched backward, his arms pinwheeling, the Smith and Wesson half drawn. A stumbling lurch, and he fell onto his back. For a few moments he shook as if afflicted with the chills, then exhaled his last and was still.

"Whooee!" Kenny exclaimed, agog. "I take back what I said before. This feller might even be faster than you, Cass!"

Cass Benedict was thoughtfully staring at the body. Going over, he nudged it with a toe and remarked, "You always were all gurgle and no guts, Mort. The one time you show some grit, and look at you."

Mort had his arms folded across his cowhide vest. "Ah well. Stupid is as stupid does, I always say. If a man's born to drown, he'll drown in a desert."

Residents of both mining camps were rushing to the scene, most armed and anticipating trouble. Slan Gheller turned to the group coming from Lodestone, raised his hands, and bellowed, "It's all right! Nothing to be alarmed about! There's been a shooting, but you can all go on about your own business!"

Arthur Nicholson was mesmerized by the corpse. He took several steps into the stream, soaking his shoes and ankles, and said in a daze, "He's dead. Honestly and truly dead."

"They get that way when they're filled with lead," Riley bantered.

"How can you joke about so hideous a deed?" the parson responded. Tearing his gaze from Mort, he whirled around. "And you, Brother Fargo! Surely you're familiar with the Ten Commandments. 'Thou shalt not kill!' How can you justify taking another being's life?"

"It was him or me," Fargo said. Sliding two cartridges from the loops on his gunbelt, he ejected the spent pair in the cylinder and replaced them.

"There had to be a better way," Arthur protested. "In Aubrick we don't allow blood to be spilled. I made that plain. 'He that smiteth a man, so that he die, shall surely be put to death'."

Slan Gheller, of all people, came to Fargo's defense. "You're not *in* Aubrick at the moment, are you, Arthur? We agreed the stream was neutral territory, remember? And you shouldn't go around threatening to put folks to death when you have no means to back it up."

"But what will my followers think?" the parson said. He surveyed the crowd from Aubrick, fifteen strong and growing. "They look up to me. They rely on me to enforce the divine dictates by which we live."

"I'll make it easy for you," Fargo offered. "I'll get my horse and go." Pivoting, he made for the onlookers, who hastily parted to let him pass. Among them, just arrived, was Amanda Nicholson, and she snatched at his arm, refusing to let him past.

"What's this? Why are you leaving?"

Fargo pointed, and she spotted Mort. A dark stain was spreading across the front of the gunman's shirt.

Her brother waded out of the water. "Your supper guest, sister, just bucked a fellow human being out in gore. He's agreed to depart, sparing us the necessity of banishing him, or worse."

"Who started it?" Amanda asked.

"That's irrelevant," the parson said. "Killing is killing, and we've agreed not to permit it under any circumstances."

Fargo tried to move on, but Amanda's grip on him

tightened. "Wait. Please," she requested. To Arthur, she said, "If he's not to blame you can't run him off."

"Listen to yourself. Time and again I've preached the consequences of sin. Time and again I've laid down punishments for infractions. What sort of shepherd would I be if I made an exception in his case? My flock requires better of me."

"He isn't *part* of your flock," Amanda said. "You can't hold him to the same standard as the rest. It wouldn't be fair."

Indecision racked Nicholson. Gnawing on his lower lip, he glanced from Fargo to the body and back again. Finally he rendered his judgment. "Very well. In the interests of fairness I'll allow Brother Fargo to stay the night. But he must leave Aubrick in the morning and promise never to return."

All their fuss was meaningless. Fargo had no intention of staying another day. He'd had his fill of the whole business. Come morning, he would gladly head out.

While the siblings argued, Slan Gheller had taken a cigar from a jacket pocket and bit off the end. Now he commented, "If they won't have you, mister, pay Lodestone a visit tomorrow. I can always use a good man with a gun." He waved the stogie at Mort. "As luck would have it, I have an opening." He let loose a hearty laugh, and Kenny, along with the others, joined in. Cass Benedict watched them in silence.

Fargo pulled his arm from Amanda's grip and walked off. Someone else could bring the two buckets. She called his name, but he kept going. At the tents he glanced back and saw her in a heated dispute with her brother. Remembering the coffee she had put on to brew, Fargo turned toward the tabernacle just in time to observe Perry Hutchings slip in through the rear door. Quickening his pace, he slunk up under the kitchen window and peered over the sill. Hutchings was nowhere in sight. Gingerly pulling on the latch, Fargo eased inside, treading softly so his spurs wouldn't jangle. Sounds from the left guided him to one of the bedrooms. Amanda's, to judge by the flowery quilt on the bed, and other feminine touches.

Perry Hutchings was at her dresser, going through drawer after drawer with great urgency. He held up a lacy undergarment, grimaced, and promptly dropped it again as if it were a cactus that had pricked his fingers.

Unnoticed Fargo leaned against the jamb. "Looking for something?"

Hutchings spun, his right hand plunging under his jacket. For a few moments they stood in awkward silence, then Hutchings's mouth curled in a lopsided, worried grin. "Mr. Fargo! You scared me half to death. I wasn't expecting anyone."

"Mind explaining what you're up to?"

"Oh. Well—I—that is—" Hutchings stuttered, and closed the drawer. "I admit this looks bad but it's not what you think."

"I'm listening," Fargo said.

Hutchings crossed the room. "How do I know I can trust you?"

"I caught you going through the Nicholsons' belongings and you're wondering if *you* can trust *me*?" Fargo almost laughed aloud at the greenhorn's gall. "You have it backwards."

"You don't understand." Hutchings tried to get by, but Fargo blocked the doorway. "If they catch me my life is in danger."

"The parson won't take kindly to a thief," Fargo agreed.

"No, it's not that. I'd never steal from anyone." Beads of sweat broke out on Hutchings's upper lip. "I was trying to find the proof I need to wrap this up. I've come so far, spent so much time and money. Now I'm close, so very close. They might have papers somewhere that will prove their guilt."

"Guilt about what?"

Hutchings glanced at the back door, then lowered his voice. "I'm from Chicago. I work for the Davis Detective Agency and I've been assigned to find—" A noise outside caused him to blanch. The next moment faint voices reached them, the voices of the parson and his sister. Uttering a low bleat, Hutchings pleaded, "Please! Let me go or I'm a dead man! I give you my word I'll explain everything later."

Fargo couldn't say why he stepped aside. Was it because he sensed Hutchings was sincere? He watched the detective dart toward the front of the church and heard his footfalls rapidly recede. The front door slammed mere seconds before the rear door opened and in walked Arthur and Amanda toting two buckets apiece.

"Here you are!" Amanda said happily. "I was worried you might have left. You're still entitled to a bath, remember?" She carried her buckets over to the stove and set them down. "How about that cup of coffee first? How would you like it?"

Fargo reclaimed his seat at the table. On the trail he always had to take his coffee black, but when the opportunity arose he liked to indulge his sweet tooth. "Five or six teaspoons of sugar would do nicely."

Grinning, Amanda retrieved a china saucer and cup from the cupboard. She poured carefully, added sugar from a small canister, and brought the steaming brew over. "Now I'll get to work filling that tub."

The fragrant aroma set Fargo's stomach to growling. Taking a sip, he smacked his lips. "Not bad." Arthur Nicholson, he noted, hadn't moved from near the back door, and was staring at him as if he had something to say. "Speak your piece."

Coughing, the parson shuffled his weight from one foot to the other. "This isn't easy for me. My sister says I overreacted. She says I should apologize for castigating you when clearly you weren't at fault. So consider this a formal apology."

"No harm done," Fargo said. "I'm planning to ride out tomorrow anyway."

Arthur and Amanda exchanged glances. "I hope it's not because of me," the former said. "I was wrong. I admit that. We would very much like for you to stay on a few more days. My sister will do all she can to make you feel right at home."

"That's right," Amanda interjected. "We'll even let you sleep here if you'd like. Pick a spot and spread out your blankets."

Fargo knew the real reason she desired to keep him around. There was a lot more to Amanda than she let on, certainly more than her brother would ever suspect. But the parson's abrupt change of heart was puzzling. "What will your flock say?" he asked him.

"I've called a special meeting tonight at nine to set things straight," Arthur said. "They're basically good, decent people. They won't hold it against me if I explain the situation to their understanding." Setting down his buckets, he slid into a chair across the table. "May I speak frankly a moment, Brother Fargo? My sister has pointed out to me that your arrival in our fair community might be a godsend in disguise."

"How would that be?" Fargo raised the cup to his lips.

"I'm a man of peace," Arthur said. "I put all my faith in the Good Book and our Maker. Usually that's enough to see us through any crisis. But against men like Slan Gheller and Cass Benedict, faith isn't always enough. Sometimes practical action is called for, action beyond my capability."

"Gheller seemed friendly enough." Unusually friendly, Fargo mused, for a man the reverend had led him to believe was a bitter enemy.

"Don't let him deceive you," Arthur responded. "He's a wily serpent, that one. As clever as a fox and as dangerous as a coiled rattler. Oh, he smiles and puts on friendly airs, but it's all a sham, a ruse to entice others into lowering their guard. Don't ever believe for a minute that he's sincere."

It was possible, Fargo supposed. He'd known killers who could gun a person down while grinning from ear to ear. But somehow Slan Gheller didn't strike him as the type. "What does all this have to do with me?"

Arthur again glanced at his sister, who nodded. Leaning across the table, he confided, "I don't trust Gheller. Oh, he agreed to leave Aubrick. But he only went to the other side of the stream and set up a new camp. He's

34

been civil enough about it, but I suspect he resents being driven out and harbors a plan to exact revenge."

"How?"

"How else? Until I came along he had everything his way. Were I to be removed, he could gain control of both mining camps. Consolidate them, perhaps, and run roughshod over everyone. For all his smiles he's a bully at heart."

Amanda jumped in. "Why else has Gheller brought in all those gunmen? Men like Cass Benedict. Men with no qualms about taking human life. They hire themselves out for one purpose and one purpose alone, to kill. Why does Gheller hire men like that unless he plans to use them for his own foul ends? And we hear more are on the way."

Fargo had to admit she had a point. Why else *was* Slan Gheller hiring a bunch of quick-draw artists? "You still haven't said what all this has to do with me."

Amanda came to the table. "My brother is no match for ruffians like Benedict. They have no fear of the Lord and contempt for Scripture. They'd shoot him down without a second thought if Gheller gave the order."

"And you want me to stick around to protect him?" Fargo deduced.

Amanda's hand enfolded his. 'Would you? Only for a short while. A few days at the most. One of our parishioners confided that he overheard a couple of Gheller's men talking about how Gheller intends to fix my brother's hash, as they phrased it, before the week is out." She squeezed his fingers. "Please, Skye. For his sake. For mine. Will you stay?"

Fargo thought of Mort, of Perry Hutchings, of the prospectors and their families, and of Amanda's glorious cleavage. "Why not? It could be interesting."

Clapping her hands, Amanda squealed for joy, rushed around, and kissed him on the cheek. Catching herself, she stepped back and said demurely, "I thank you from the bottom of my heart."

"We both do," the parson said.

The very next moment there was a timid knock at the

back door. Arthur rose to answer it. Fargo couldn't see who was outside from where he sat, but he heard a woman, possibly middle-aged or older.

"Sorry to disturb you, Preacher."

"Why, Sister Williams. How nice to see you again. What's brought you here?" Arthur cheerfully asked.

"I brought our tithe," the woman said.

Fargo saw the parson reach out and accept something from her.

"For which I heartily thank you." Arthur oozed charm. "If only the rest of my flock were as conscientious as you and your husband. Sad to say, but some are a month or more behind."

"Ah shucks," Mrs. Williams said. "We're just doing our part. We know how much you count on these tithes for the new church you want to build, and all the rest of the wonderful plans you have for Aubrick."

"You are a credit to your Maker, sister. The Lord willing, a year or so from now we'll have a thriving town, with nice homes for everyone. There will be a bank and all kinds of business establishments. And a new tabernacle, one with solid walls so the wind doesn't chill us in cold weather. And comfortable pews for everyone to sit in."

"Don't forget that nice house for your charming sister and you," Mrs. Williams said. "You deserve a place of your own."

"Only after all the rest of our community's needs have been met," Arthur said. "Your welfare and comfort must always come before ours."

"Dang if you don't bring a lump to my throat, Parson. I reckon you're just about the most noble fella I ever did meet. And I'm not the only one who thinks so. Most everybody can't praise you highly enough. You're doing a wonderful job."

"It warms my soul to hear that, sister. Now if you'll excuse me, I have some work I must attend to." Arthur started to close the door.

"One more thing, Parson. Something I thought you ought to know." Mrs. Williams's voice dropped to a loud whisper. "On my way over I saw that fella who was asking all those questions about you—"

"Perry Hutchings?"

"That's the one. He came bolting out of the front of your church like his britches were on fire."

"When was this?" Arthur inquired, his cheerful demeanor gone.

"Oh, not five minutes ago. It got me curious, so I followed him to see what he was up to. He went to his tent, and I figured he'd be there a while. I was about to come here when he scooted off again, all in a hurry, and headed across the stream."

"To Lodestone?"

"Yes, sir. I spied on him and saw him go into Slan Gheller's place." Mrs. Williams paused. "Just thought it might be important."

"My dear woman, you have no idea."

Fargo could tell the parson was extremely upset but trying hard not to show it. Amanda, too, took the news grimly. It gave the impression they knew more about Hutchings than they let on.

"I'll keep my eyes and ears open, like you wanted," Mrs. Williams stated. "All us ladies will. If this Hutchings fella is causing you trouble, you just say the word and we'll have our menfolk run him out on a rail."

"That won't be necessary, I assure you. Remember, we're to love our neighbors, not abuse them."

Mrs. Williams wasn't done. "He's a fishy character, that one. Skulking around like he does, always prying into your doings. Audie told me that he was badgering her about whether you ever mentioned being in Chicago."

"Chicago? No, I haven't. I wonder why he thinks that's so important."

"Beats me, Parson. But he's up to no good. I feel it in my bones. And after all the swell things you've done, and all the big plans you have, we're not going to allow him or anyone else to cause you and your sweet sister any grief. You hear?"

"Yes," Arthur said absently, gripping the latch again.

"Please convey my regards to your husband. And thank your sisters for their able assistance. Now, I really must go." He shut the door and walked toward the table, deep in thought. In his left hand was a small poke.

"The more we learn about Hutchings, the less I like," Amanda remarked.

"I should banish him," Arthur said.

"For what? Asking a lot of questions? Don't be silly. You'll need more justification than that or—" Amanda stopped and glanced at Fargo. "Listen to me prattle. For a second there I almost forgot you were here."

Arthur blinked, then went to shove the poke into his pocket, but changed his mind and dropped it on the table instead.

Fargo didn't hear the clatter of coins or nuggets. "Gold dust?" he speculated.

"I made an appeal to those who are able to help support our ministry as best they can," Arthur said defensively. "Tithing is a long-established church tradition. How else are men like me to make ends meet? We don't ask a lot, just enough to get by. Is that so wrong? Look around you. It's not as if I'm extorting the gold from them, and I—"

Fargo held up a hand and the parson hushed. "I wasn't accusing you of anything."

"Oh." Arthur looked at his sister, who grinned, gripped him by the shoulders, and steered him toward the door. "Quit blathering and go see if they have that gunman's grave dug yet. You agreed to preside over the burial service, didn't you? They'll be expecting you shortly."

"That's right. Thanks for reminding me."

"Aren't you forgetting something?" Fargo asked.

Brother and sister stopped, perplexed. Arthur glanced at the poke, bounded back, and palmed the drawstring. "I don't know where my mind is today."

Fargo pointed at the Bible. "I meant that."

"See what I mean? I guess the shooting and this Hutchings business have me more flustered than I thought," the parson said sheepishly. Reverently picking it up, he pressed it to his chest. 'Forgive me."

"There's nothing to forgive," Fargo said, and Arthur hastened off. But he couldn't help thinking how strange it was the parson showed more concern for the gold than the Good Book. And what was it about Perry Hutchings that had the Nicholsons so disturbed? He wasn't given much chance to ponder either issue because the moment the door closed behind her brother, Amanda sashayed toward him grinning like a cat about to devour a mouse.

"He'll be gone a good long while, handsome. So why don't I fill the tub and you can shed those buckskins." Pursing her red lips, Amanda came around the table and placed her hands on his shoulders. "Ask me real nice and I might even help you undress."

4

Skye Fargo swiveled in his chair, wrapped his left arm around Amanda Nicholson's hips, and, pulling her close, buried his face against her dress at the junction of her thighs. A startled "Oh!" escaped her as he kissed her through the fabric, and her fingers locked at the nape of his neck to hold him in place.

"You are *so* naughty!" Amanda exclaimed. "I'm tingling all over."

Fargo was just getting started. He kissed a path up across her flat stomach to her marvelous twin mounds and applied his mouth to her left breast. It swelled outward, and he teased the nipple with his tongue, leaving a moist spot. Amanda wriggled deliciously, then tugged him out of the chair and glued her body to his. Her lips were molten honey, her tongue flowing nectar. Their kiss lingered for minutes without end until she broke it and stepped back, flushed from neck to brow, her eyes dilated with passion, her nostrils flared with desire.

"I want you so badly."

Fargo shared her hunger, but he didn't care to have her brother or a parishioner blunder in on them. So, his arm around her slender waist, he moved her toward her bedroom. She offered no resistance. Indeed, after the first couple of steps, she went faster and pulled him along, her mouth curled in temptress invitation.

The bed was a modest four-poster, the flowery quilt as soft as grass. Amanda sank onto her back, her fingers locked on his arms so he had no choice but to follow

40

her example. She gave his hat a toss, then attacked his belt buckle with an eagerness bordering on ferocity.

"What's your hurry?" Fargo asked, shifting onto his side. "You said your brother will be gone a while." He preferred to indulge in some foreplay before battering at the gate. Experience had taught him that lovemaking, like stew, should be brought to a slow boil, the better to savor the end result.

The buckle was giving Amanda trouble and she expressed a few unladylike swear words, finishing with, "I told you before. It's been ages since a man kissed me, ages since I felt that special feeling deep inside."

"Let me," Fargo said, and undid the buckle himself. Hardly had the belt fallen to the quilt than she attacked his pants, undoing them with a speed he would find daunting to match. He didn't quite know what she intended until, wearing a triumphant grin, she plunged a hand down his pants and boldly gripped his hardening pole.

"Ahhhhhh," Amanda cooed, gently stroking him.

Fargo's manhood grew rigid as iron. His breath caught in his throat, and a warm sensation spread upward from his loins. Her fingers elicited exquisite sensations magnified by the attention her mouth and tongue were giving his neck.

Amanda looked up, womanly lust incarnate. "You're bigger than most in more ways than one, aren't you?"

The constriction in Fargo's throat prevented him from answering. He wrapped his fingers in her silken hair as she ran her warm tongue from his shoulder to his left ear. Her warm breath caressed him, her hand cupped him low down. He almost exploded prematurely. It took every ounce of concentration he possessed to contain himself.

Amanda pushed him onto his back and straddled his thighs with her own. Her dress hiked to her hips, revealing superbly shaped legs as creamy as milk. Not once did she lose her grip on his member, and when she was on top, she stroked him harder, faster. Her mouth swooped to his, and fused, as she began a slight rocking motion. Her breasts brushed his chest with each movement.

Usually Fargo took the initiative when it came to bedroom dalliances. But Amanda's undeniable need had rendered her the aggressor, which was fine by him. Either way, the end result was the same.

"Ohhhhh. You have me so hot," Amanda mentioned between kisses. "So wet."

"Really?" Fargo said, and slid a hand up under her dress. Deftly parting her undergarments, he made contact with an inner thigh. It was as smooth as glass. She trembled at his touch, and moaned. His forefinger rose higher to rub her dripping slit, and she arched her back.

"Yes! Oh, yes!"

Fargo inserted the tip of his finger and slid it from front to back. Amanda moaned louder and closed her eyes, but not for long. They shot wide open when his finger delicately flicked her swollen knob, and her grip on his pole increased to where it was almost painful.

"I'm so close!" Amanda breathed. "So very close!"

Fargo wasn't, not by a long shot. He slowly inserted his finger into her womanhood and the next moment had a wildcat to contend with. Amanda erupted in a heaving paroxysm, bucking so ferociously he had to grip her waist with his other hand to keep her from slipping off. At the selfsame moment she threw her head back and gave voice to a loud, long cry of utter and total abandon.

Sliding his finger almost out, Fargo rammed it in to the knuckle. He was holding Amanda firmly enough, he thought, to keep her in place. But he wasn't counting on the violence of her reaction. She heaved toward the ceiling as if fired by a canon, a banshee shriek rising from her throat. A shriek she smothered by clamping her teeth shut, although not before her cry filled the room and perhaps the church.

Fargo's finger slid out. He lost his grip. Amanda dropped back onto him, and with dire urgency, as if her life were in the bargain, she exposed his pole, aligned herself above it, and fed him into her hot, wet core. Not by gradual degrees as most women would do, but all at once, virtually impaling herself on his member. She shrieked again as his full steely length was sheathed by her velvet scabbard. This time she shoved her forearm over her mouth, but it didn't completely dampen her outburst.

Fargo held himself still, permitting Amanda to set the tempo, which she did after grabbing a pillow and cramming a corner into her mouth. Wheezing like a bellows, she swung her hips forward and back, grinding into him in a frenzy. Her inner walls rippled and contracted nonstop. Her thighs closed on his hips, seeking added purchase. She pumped back and forth in perpetual motion, and with each forward thrust she screeched in violent ecstasy. The pillow dampened her outcries to a degree, but Fargo had to wonder if anyone passing by might hear her, jump to the conclusion she was being molested, and barge inside.

Suddenly Amanda's eyes grew their widest yet. Paradoxically she fell quiet, but only for a few seconds. For as her voluptuous body went into spasms of release and her womanhood unclosed him like a glove, she screamed in total delirium. Her head thrashed from side to side, her body arched like a bowstring, and she slammed against him as if striving to drive him through the bed.

Fargo intended to hold out longer, to treat himself to several more minutes of unquenched pleasure. But her release spontaneously triggered his own, ripping from him the explosion he had so far successfully checked. Clasping Amanda to him, he spread up into her with redoubled vigor. The combined tumult of their frenzied exertions started the four-poster to thumping against the floor.

The pillow fell from Amanda's mouth and she cried out, "Ah! Ah! Again! I'm coming again!"

The room around Fargo blurred. The hammering of his pulse eclipsed the hammering of the bedposts. He was carried aloft as if by an inner wave of sensual sensation and cast adrift on a sea of physical bliss. He came and came, and came again. For what seemed like an interminable interval he floated in a twilight realm of

43

pure delight, only to be jarred back to the land of the living by Amanda, who collapsed against him, her cheek on his throat, her bosom cushioned by his sternum.

"I never . . . I never . . ." Amanda couldn't finish her statement. Exhausted, her hair and clothes disheveled, she tried to lift a hand to touch his face but lacked the strength.

Fargo rolled her onto her side and she closed her eyes, on the verge of dozing off. But not him. Raising his head, he listened for any suggestion they had been overheard. The only sound was the ticking of a clock.

Easing onto his back, Fargo yawned. He could use a nap, but try as he might he couldn't fall asleep. The events of the day had wound his nerves as tight as barbed wire. He reviewed them, starting with his run-in with Bethany Mackenzie and all that happened up to his last talk with the parson. Of particular interest was Perry Hutchings. The detective knew something about the Nicholsons, something that had them greatly flustered. Since he'd agreed to stay with them a few days, it might prove worthwhile to find Hutchings and get to the bottom of whatever the man was up to.

The clock on the wall indicated Fargo still had an hour and a half before supper. Since sleeping was out of the question, he quietly rose, hitched up his pants, and buckled on his gun belt. Donning his hat, he made for the back door. He left the Henry propped against the wall.

A small crowd, mostly women, had gathered at a spot approximately twenty yards northeast of the stream, on the Aubrick side. The earthly remains of Mort had been wrapped in a dirty, tattered canvas, and lay at the lip of a deep hole. Arthur had availed himself of the opportunity to deliver a sermon, and as Fargo passed by, unnoticed, the parson was expounding on the "dire harvest reaped by those who break the Commandments."

Only one person from Lodestone had bothered to show up: Cass Benedict. Benedict stood aloof from the rest, his hat respectfully in hand. Always alert, he spotted Fargo, stared a moment, and nodded.

Fargo repaid the show of respect. He didn't quite

know what to make of the short gunfighter. Like Slan Gheller, Benedict's actions didn't match his reputation. But then, that wasn't unusual. Gossip, rumor, and newspaper accounts were all the same. Facts were always distorted. People were portrayed as much worse than they turned out to be. Fargo should know. His exploits had been written about a score of times. The only thing was little of what had been committed to paper had any basis in fact.

The gazettes were the worst. "Dreadfuls," some folks called them, and Fargo had to agree. Cranked out by hack writers who never let the truth get in the way of a rollicking good story, they presented a totally false picture of life in the West. Violent scrapes with hostile Indians were turned into glorious epics of frontier bravery. Outlaws were presented as latter-day Robin Hoods. Gunmen had their tallies embellished dramatically. A man who shot two or three might find himself credited with twenty or thirty.

Rags like *Harper's Weekly, Leslie's Weekly,* and the *Police Gazette* were the three most widely read. Fifty-two weeks a year they churned out outrageous lies in the guise of genuine fact. Copies could be found in every tavern, saloon, barbershop, and general store across the country. In large cities back East every new edition was hawked on street corners by kids bawling out the latest lurid headlines.

Much to Fargo's annoyance he was a favorite subject. Like Bridger and Carson before him, the gazettes had taken a special interest in his career. When they couldn't come up with factual accounts, which they then exaggerated out of all proportion, they made things up out of whole cloth. They put him in places he had never been, doing things he had never done. One week a writer had him in Alaska, slaying a Kodiak bear with a butcher knife. The next week they had him in Mexico fighting a lost tribe of Aztecs.

The first time Fargo saw a gazette story about himself, he'd laughed. Who wouldn't? It had been a trifle, something about him saving a "maiden fair" from a "vile pack of renegade Pawnatucks." Never mind that it never happened. Never mind that there was no such tribe. The writer had presented him as a "noble son of the prairie, as courageous as Achilles, as handsome as Hamlet, as strong as Thor." Fargo hadn't seen how anyone could take it seriously, which showed how badly he had misjudged human nature. Readers loved the tales, and the writers capitalized by presenting one lurid escapade after another.

Fargo often wished he could round up all the writers who had done his life an injustice and hand them over to the Apaches. A few hours of reality would do wonders for their craft.

On reaching the stream Fargo looked for a shallow spot to cross. Someone else had gone him one better, and fifteen yards to the south large stones had been placed at regular intervals from bank to bank. By hopping from one to the other he reached the west side.

From a distance Lodestone appeared to be Aubrick's twin, but the two mining camps were very different. Lodestone only had half as many tents. Few women were in evidence, and no children whatsoever. It said a lot about human nature that those who built the saloon clearly took more pride in their work than those who had constructed the church. Made entirely of logs, the *Aces High,* as Gheller had named it, was an oasis of elegance in a wasteland of grime. Glass windows kept out the dust and wind. The hardwood floor was swept clean, and spittoons were common. Green felt tablecloths covered the tables. On two walls hung large paintings of naked women in seductive poses. Stools lined the bar, and behind it hung a wide mirror etched along the border with pink roses.

Fargo paused just inside the batwing doors. The place was packed. Cigar and cigarette smoke hung as thick as mist. Half a dozen poker games were underway, and a roulette wheel was being spun by a dealer in a crisp suit. The tiger was being bucked by gamblers oblivious to the rest of the world. Nine or ten full-bodied women in tight dresses mingled with the customers, enticing them to spend more of their hard-earned money.

They couldn't *all* be from Lodestone, Fargo realized. The good people of Aubrick weren't as vice-free as Arthur made them out to be. Shouldering through the onlookers to the bar, he spied a long shelf crammed with every kind of liquor known to man; Scotch, bourbon, brandy, and more. Grinning, he smacked the counter to get the bartender's attention, and said, "Whiskey. The best you've got. And leave the bottle."

To his left someone coughed. "If you don't mind my saying so, you look like a gent who just discovered heaven on earth."

Fargo swiveled, his right elbow on the counter, his hand inches from the Colt. Slan Gheller was puffing on a thick cigar, ringlets of gray smoke wreathing his white hat. Riley and Kenny flanked him, watchful but not threatening. "If you don't mind my saying so," Fargo mimicked, "you sound a lot like the parson."

Gheller laughed and bellied closer. Patrons automatically moved aside to give him however much room he needed, and the bartender, without being asked, brought Gheller a glass of brandy before pouring Fargo's whiskey.

"To Arthur, and his deal with the devil," Gheller said, raising his glass in a toast. With a single gulp he drained the contents.

"What deal would that be?" Fargo asked.

"Haven't you heard? He agreed to leave me in peace so long as I removed myself from his precious flock." Gheller grinned. "You wouldn't guess it to look at him, but Arthur has more sand than most ten men."

"You almost sound as if you admire him."

"I admire anyone who can get away with what he has," Gheller said matter-of-factly. "You don't know him like I do."

Fargo took a swallow, mulling over whether Lodestone's leading citizen was sincere. "You don't resent the fact that he drove you out of Aubrick?"

"Look around you." Gheller gestured at the standing-room-only throng. "Did it hurt my business any? Quite the opposite. Before, a lot of the men stayed away for fear of being seen by their wives. Now, they can sneak over here without their wives being any the wiser, so they come more often. Half these yokels are supposed to be off working claims, but they'd rather be having a good time."

That they were. As Fargo observed, most were smiling and laughing, and thoroughly enjoying themselves. He recognized more than a few faces from Aubrick, among them Lon Wolgast and his friends.

"Hell, Arthur did me a favor by kicking me out," Gheller said. "I'm making more money now than I ever did across the stream."

Kenny cackled. "The Bible thumper should get a cut of the profits, huh, boss?" he said, and winked.

Slan Gheller didn't find the comment the least bit funny. Suddenly pivoting, he backhanded his young underling across the cheek. Kenny was sent stumbling, more embarrassed than hurt.

Fargo wasn't sure why Gheller had done it. He half expected the young gunman to resort to his hardware, but Kenny merely grinned and elevated both hands to show there were no hard feelings.

"One of these days that loose tongue of yours will be the death of you," Slan Gheller said sternly.

"I didn't mean anything by it, boss, honest."

Riley rolled his eyes to the ceiling. "You're an idiot, kid. You know Mr. Gheller doesn't let anyone talk about the parson except him."

Fargo wondered why that should be. Maybe their employer has a secret religious streak, and was one of those who didn't let others speak ill of anyone doing the Lord's work.

Gheller pointed at a corner table, the only empty table in the saloon. "How about the two of us have a private palaver? I have a few questions I'd like to ask. My boys will stay here." Taking it for granted Fargo would agree, he walked toward it.

Fargo had no objections. He had a few questions of his own he'd like to pose. Taking the bottle, he followed.

While others had to shoulder their way through the throng, a clear path materialized for Slan Gheller as if by arcane magic. A bear among wolves, he was treated with respect, even a degree of fear. He sat so he could survey the room, removed his white hat, and set it on the table. "This is exclusively reserved for me," he mentioned.

Fargo sat so his back was to a wall. Refilling his glass, he looked for the person he had come there to find. "Do you know Perry Hutchings?"

"I've seen him around," Gheller said evasively.

"He was spotted coming in here less than an hour ago," Fargo remarked.

"So?" Gheller shrugged. "People are constantly coming and going. I don't keep track of them. Especially dandies from back East who make a nuisance of themselves asking a lot of damned fool question."

"About the Nicholsons?"

"About a lot of things," Gheller said gruffly, "including you. He'd heard of you, but he couldn't quite place where until I mentioned that name they call you in the gazettes. The Trailsman. When he found out who you are, he mumbled something about making a terrible mistake and left without another word. He's downright peculiar, that one. Where he ran off to I have no idea."

Fargo had hoped to keep his identity quiet. "So he came to you for information?"

"Why is that so strange? I'm top dog hereabouts, in case you haven't noticed. Running this place as I do, I learn a lot of things about a lot of people. He thought I might know something useful."

It made sense, Fargo reflected. Saloons were the social hub of every town and mining camp, for the men, at any rate. Alcohol loosened their lips as well as their pockets, and they said things they shouldn't, secrets better kept to themselves, information they would never share if they were sober. "Did Hutchings mention why he's so interested in the parson and his sister?"

49

"No. And I don't rightly care. After the second or third question I told him to go stick his head up a horse's ass." Gheller leaned on his elbows. "Now how about you leveling with me? What are you doing in a two-bit drop of spit like Aubrick?"

"Passing through."

"Then you don't' plan to stick around?" The prospect made Gheller smile.

"I wasn't going to until the Nicholsons begged me." Fargo lifted his glass, and over it saw a fleeting scowl ripple across his host's face.

"Why would they do that?" Gheller asked, then grinned knowingly. "Oh. I get it. It's the sister's doing. Amanda has taken a shine to you, eh? Between you and me, that gal has as powerful a hankering for men as her brother supposedly has for the Good Book."

"They asked me to stick around to protect them from you." Fargo revealed the truth both as a warning, and to test the reaction he'd get.

Slan Gheller hove up out of his chair as if fit to lunge across the table. He darkened from the neck up, a thunderclap about to burst, his bushy brows pinching together like ominous storm clouds colliding. "That's what they told you?" he roared. "They see me as a threat?" His bellow silenced half the room, and everyone within earshot turned. Riley and Kenny started over from the bar but were stopped by a curt slash of their employer's hand. Gheller slowly sank back down, his fists clenching and unclenching. After a while, after the hubbub of conversation resumed and none of the customers were looking his way, he asked in a raspy growl, "You're not trying to hoodwink me?"

"Why would I?" Fargo rejoined. "What would I stand to gain?" He treated himself to more whiskey. "I came over to tell you stay away from them. If anything happens, if their church is burnt down or a horse spooks and tramples the parson or his sister, you'll answer to me." Fargo doubted Gheller would try gunning the parson down or having his throat slit, not when Aubrick's citizens were bound to rise up in righteous wrath. Murdering a woman was even worse. On the frontier harming a female was a guaranteed death sentence. So if Gheller intended to eliminate them, he had to make their deaths appear to be an accident.

"That miserable—" Gheller said, and gnashed his teeth together. "I don't reckon you'll believe me, but they're lying through their teeth. It wouldn't be in my best interests to harm either of them."

Fargo gazed out over the bustling activity. He had to admit Gheller had a point. It would be stupid to jeopardize a business venture reaping money hand over proverbial fist, and Gheller wasn't stupid.

"Did they give a reason why I'd want to make maggot bait of them?"

"Revenge, mainly," Fargo said.

Gheller uttered a contemptuous laugh. "Revenge for doing me the biggest favor they ever could have done? You saw me at the stream earlier. Did I act as if I hated them?"

Before Fargo could respond, Gheller gave a start and glanced past him. Twisting, Fargo set eyes on a woman who had come up on them unseen. Not one of the lovelies in skimpy outfits but a stout keg of a female in her late fifties or early sixties. Her face was creased with wrinkles, her long hair a stark gray, but she radiated a vitality women half her age seldom displayed. She was dressed in a clean homespun shirt and loose pants, and she was holding a Sharps rifle pointed at the lord of Lodestone.

"Marjorie," Gheller said. "To what do I owe this honor?"

Fargo recollected hearing that name before. Marjorie Mackenzie was the mother of Bethany Mackenzie, the young raven-tressed beauty who had been running from Cass Benedict's bunch.

"Spare me your sour sweet talk, you snake in the grass," was her reply. "My girl told me what happened today. I have half a mind to blow out your wick where you sit."

"Now you hold on there, old lady," Gheller said. "I haven't done anything wrong."

"First off, I'm not a lady, and I ain't half as old as my ma when she went to her reward," Marjorie said testily. "Second of all, I told you before to leave my girl be. But this mornin', when she was out huntin' deer, your jackals spotted her and gave chase—"

"Only to ask if she was ready to accept my standing invitation for the two of you to join me for supper some evening," Gheller broke in. "You know how I feel about your daughter. Do you honestly think I'd harm her?"

The mother took another step. "You're a lecher, Slan Gheller, pure and simple. And you'll have no truck with my girl, not now, not ever." She glanced at Fargo. "Who are you, mister? Another of this galoot's gunnies?"

"No," Fargo said. He felt no need to elaborate.

Marjorie's green eyes narrowed. "You're a liar. Beth told me about a fella she ran into today and you fit the description." She swung the Sharps toward him. "I hate liars. Maybe I should put a bullet into you so Gheller will take the hint." She thumbed back the hammer. "Any last words?"

5

Skye Fargo took Marjorie Mackenzie seriously. Frontier women were a hardy breed, as different from their daintier cousins back East as cougars were from house cats. They could ride, they could shoot, they could live off the land as well as any man. They could kill when they had to. And most were fine shots, able to hit an apple on a fence post at thirty yards. In short, they were as tough as gristle.

Fargo had no doubts Marjorie fully intended to do what she claimed. But he didn't try to snatch the rifle. She wasn't quite close enough to reach before she fired. Nor did he try to jump aside. It might provoke her into shooting that much sooner. Instead, he smiled, looked her in the eyes, and said, "You won't kill me."

Marjorie raised her cheek from the Sharps. "What makes you so damn sure?"

"You're not a killer at heart. All I did was talk to your daughter." Fargo jerked a thumb at Slan Gheller. "I don't work for him. I never have, I never will."

Gheller spoke up without being addressed. "Think what you will of me, Marjorie. But everyone knows I'm a man of my word. I have a lot of vices, but lying isn't one of them. He's playing straight with you. This here is the Trailsman. Maybe you've heard of him?"

"Can't say as I have, no," Marjorie said. A moment more she held the Sharps level, then she slowly lowered the muzzle a couple of inches. "But I still don't trust you," she told Fargo. "You sittin' here like you are, all nice and cozy with this polecat. Maybe you don't work for him, but any fool can see you're right friendly."

Gheller roared with mirth.

"What tickled your funny bone?" Marjorie angrily demanded.

"You wouldn't believe me if I told you," Gheller replied, and bobbed his head at an empty chair. "Do me the honor of joining us for a while. Please. I want to set you straight on a few things."

"You've got that backward, polecat," Marjorie said. She plunked down, though, the Sharps in front of her, her finger never leaving the trigger. "I'll do you the courtesy of hearin' you out, then you'll do the same for me."

Gheller didn't waste a second. "It's no secret I'm fond of Bethany. From the very first minute I saw her, she's all I ever think about, all I dream about. I can't say why. I only know I want to get to know her better."

"Is that all?" Marjorie goaded when he paused.

"No. You need to understand how I feel. I could never hurt her, not in a million years." Gheller placed his hands flat, palms up. "I beg you, Widow Mackenzie. Give me a chance to prove myself. Accept my invitation to dinner. Get to know me and you'll see I'd make a fine suitor."

"You're lookin' to marry my girl?"

"Who can say? We must get to know one another first. Maybe she won't like me as much as I do her, in which case we'll go our separate ways and that will be that." Slan Gheller grinned. "That should prove my intentions are sincere."

"All it proves is that you must think I'm dumber than the south end of a northbound mule," Marjorie countered. "Beth is the apple of my eye. She's as innocent as new rain, as honest as the year is long. Pairin' her up with you would be like mixin' gold and hog slop."

Gheller was offended but he asked politely, "What is it you have against me, exactly, Widow Mackenzie?"

"Where to begin?" Marjorie surveyed the saloon. "You run a house of loose morals. You're a gambler. You drink to excess. You hire womenfolk to flaunt their bodies as if they're displays in a store window. You surround yourself with trigger fanners." She faced him. "I could go on and on but why bother. You're despicable, is what you are. I'd sooner see my girl take up with a patent medicine salesman."

"You make it sound as if I'm scum."

Marjorie smirked. "You're beginnin' to get the idea. You're just lucky my Finnian ain't alive. He'd have blown our your wick for dàrin' to think you're worthy of our sweet Bethany."

Fargo saw Gheller's lips compress.

"You still blame me for his death, don't you? You still think I had something to do with it?"

Rather than answer him directly, the old woman turned to Fargo. "My husband was murdered. Shot in the back not one week after this no-account and his pack of vermin showed up. This lecher here would have me believe it was coincidence. But I know he had an argument with my Fin the day before Fin was killed."

"I've explained all that," Gheller said in exasperation. "Your husband wanted me to extend him credit on two or three small nuggets he had with him so he could sit in on a poker game. But he wanted more credit than I was willing to give so he got hot under the collar. That's all there was to it."

"My Fin never gambled a day in his life," Marjorie said stiffly. "And I'll thank you not to besmirch his memory with your lies." Rising, she cradled the Sharps. "This is your last warning, Slan Gheller. Keep away from my girl. Keep your men away from her, too. If'n you don't, I'll carve you a new navel with hot lead."

"Marjorie—" Gheller said, but Mackenzie wasn't listening. She went a few steps, then turned for one last broadside.

"Don't think you're off the hook about Fin, neither. I can't prove you had him killed, not yet anyhow, but I will, and when I do I'll come a-gunnin' for your wretched hide." Her spine a ramrod, she marched out, pushing a few patrons who didn't get out of her way fast enough to suit her.

Gheller sighed and replaced his hat. "This is some day

I'm having. First you waltz in here and threaten me, then that old she-bear. At the rate I'm going, I'll be lucky to be alive come midnight." He glanced toward the bar, toward Riley and Kenny, and jerked his head toward the batwing doors. Both gunmen immediately put down their drinks and hastened toward it.

Unfurling, Fargo slid back his chair. "How much for the whiskey?"

"It's on the house." Gheller also stood. "One last thing before you go. Don't believe everything the parson tells you. He's not the saint he makes himself out to be."

"Who is?" Fargo said, and left. He had been given a lot more to think about, but at the moment he was more concerned for Marjorie Mackenzie. She was forty yards away, striding swiftly. Riley and Kenny were just past the corner of the saloon, marking her progress from under their hats. When she disappeared around a tent Riley nudged the younger gunman and they hurried after her. Fargo had no idea what they were up to, but he didn't like it. He shadowed them, which wasn't difficult to do since they never thought to look back.

Marjorie skipped across the stream on the large stones. Shying wide of Aubrick, she bore to the northeast, skirted the camp, and made a beeline for the forested hills overlooking the valley, the same hills Bethany had disappeared into earlier.

Riley and Kenny hung far back enough to ensure they wouldn't lose sight of her. When she was a goodly distance past the mining camp she turned to check behind her, but as luck would have it, both gunmen were screened by a thicket and she didn't spot them.

Wrongly convinced she was safe, Marjorie hiked on, headed for the tree line. She exhibited the agility of a mountain goat, ascending the steep slopes with casual ease.

Fargo began to narrow the gap. He didn't owe the Mackenzies a thing, but he'd never been one to stand idly by when a woman, or most anyone else, was in possible danger. It had become a habit; it was responsible for getting him into more shooting scrapes and other unpleasant situations than he cared to count. But he couldn't help himself. People in need sparked within him an urge to help. Why he did it was as much a mystery to him as it was to his friends, some of whom had told him to his face he was a fool to stick his neck out for people he hardly knew. Maybe so, but Fargo could no more stop lending a helping hand than he could stop himself from being attracted to pretty women.

Marjorie was almost to the pines. Her stamina was extraordinary; she hadn't stopped to catch her breath once.

The same couldn't be said of Riley and Kenny. Accustomed to relying on horses to go any great distance, they quickly grew winded. As they negotiated a winding gully that would bring them out near where Marjorie Mackenzie had disappeared into the pines, they were huffing and puffing like steam engines.

By then Fargo was only twenty yards behind the pair, on the gully rim to their left. Darting from boulder to boulder, he bided his time, waiting for the right moment to show himself. They halted, and Kenny scrambled up to the right rim to peek out and verify the old woman was nowhere near. He beckoned to Riley. They had to move swiftly or they would lose sight of her.

Fargo lowered his hand to his Colt. Not to shoot them but to persuade them to turn back. At daybreak he would return alone and follow Marjorie's tracks to the Mackenzie place. He'd like to see Bethany again and learn more about the death of her father. But as he started to straighten, there she was, appearing out of nowhere, her Spencer wedged to her shoulder and trained on the two gunnies.

"That's as far as you go."

Riley and Kenny were caught flat-footed halfway up the gully. Riley held his hands out from his sides, but Kenny instinctively reached for his revolver.

"You do," Bethany warned, "and they'll plant you beside your friend Mort before this day is done." As gorgeous as ever, the floppy hat hid her green eyes but not her mocking smile.

"You know about Mort, missy?" Riley said.

"From up here we can see everything that goes on down yonder," Bethany responded. "All the comings and goings. All the folks who sneak about at all hours of the day and night." She paused. "Take you two, for instance. I figured it'd be a smart notion to watch my ma's back trail. I knew your boss would send someone to plug her."

Kenny had all the tact of a lump of coal. "Hell, you've got it all wrong, stupid. We're not out to backshoot your ma. Mr. Gheller wouldn't harm a gray hair on her head 'cause it might rile you."

"Then why are you shadowin' her?"

"To find out where the two of you hole up," Kenny replied. "Everybody knows you live off in these hills somewhere, but no one knows exactly where. Mr. Gheller would give anything to know. He'd like to come courting."

"How dumb do you think I am?" Bethany sneered.

"He's telling the truth, missy," Riley said. "The boss called all of us into the saloon the other day and told us to keep our eyes skinned. That if we saw you or your ma down in the valley, we're to trail you. Whoever finds your homestead gets a hundred-dollar bonus."

"I could sure use that money," Kenny said. "I need me some new boots, and I've got my heart set on a pearl-handled Colt." He took a half step higher. "But I'm not greedy. Tell us where your cabin is and I'll cut you in for twenty dollars. What do you say?"

"I'd rather wallow in elk droppings than make a deal with the likes of you." Bethany hefted the Spencer. "Now turn around, make like the coyotes you are, and skulk on out of here."

Riley complied, but Kenny didn't budge. "How about thirty dollars? That's more money than a gal like you probably sees in a whole year. Think of all the fine foolery you could buy, dresses and combs and such."

"We don't need no paltry thirty dollars," Bethany said haughtily. "We have plenty of go—" She caught herself, but the slip had not gone unnoticed.

The two gunmen traded looks, then headed down.

Kenny glanced back every now and again as if in dread of being shot in the back, but Riley showed no fear at all.

Fargo saw Bethany gnaw on her lower lip. She fully realized, he suspected, the blunder she had made. But short of murdering the two hardcases, what else could she do? She stared after them until they were at the base of the hill, then she spun and darted into the forest. As fleet as an antelope, fluid grace in motion, she raced to catch up with her mother.

Fargo finally straightened. He committed the spot where she had entered the trees to memory, and headed down himself. The sun was perched on the western horizon. Soon it would relinquish the heavens to the stars. The Nicholsons would be sitting down to supper any time now, and it was one meal he did not care to miss.

Weary prospectors were filing toward Aubrick from the north end of the creek. In twos and threes they trudged to their tents, some to be welcomed by wives and children, others to spruce themselves up and head for Lodestone.

The Ovaro was dozing at the front of the church. Fargo unwound the reins from the nail and led the stallion around to the rear. Undoing the cinch, he removed his saddle and took off the saddle blanket and bridle. Inside, Amanda was laughing. He unwound his rope, looped one end over the pinto's neck, and secured the other to a tree stump. Hoisting the saddle and blanket onto his shoulder, he knocked on the door. Amanda admitted him. The tantalizing aroma of cooking food made his mouth water.

"Brother Fargo!" she exclaimed. "We were wondering where in the world you got to!" A light green dress clung to her body where dresses should cling, and she had recently washed her hair.

"I've been around," Fargo said. He was surprised to see Perry Hutchings already at the table, as was the parson. Hutchings had on the same brown suit, and the bowler was on a peg behind him. A white cloth covered the table. Fine silverware had been laid out, along with cloth napkins and four glasses of water. In the center was a silver candleholder in which three white candles glowed.

"There you are!" Arthur said, rising. "I was becoming worried. Someone mentioned they saw you go to Lodestone."

Fargo deposited the saddle, blanket, and bridle in the same corner as the Henry. His hat went on a peg next to the bowler, and he straddled a chair.

Perry Hutchings had a pinch-faced aspect, as if he were seated on a railroad spike. "I just arrived a couple of minutes ago myself," he said. "Miss Nicholson tells me we're having a meal fit for King Solomon."

"Courtesy of some of the wives," Amanda said from over at the stove. Two large pots and pans were on the griddles, and a loaf of fresh bread was on the counter, half a dozen slices cut and ready. "They are such dears. When they heard I was having a special meal, they all contributed."

"Truly the salt of the earth," the parson intoned.

Perry Hutchings looked down at the table.

"So tell us all about your afternoon," Amanda coaxed Fargo. "Since you were gone so long, I used the bath water myself. Hope you don't mind."

"What did you do across the stream?" her brother asked.

"I had a long talk with Slan Gheller," Fargo disclosed. "He wasn't very pleased when I told him to stay away from you."

Arthur was shocked. "You did what?"

"You asked me to protect you," Fargo reminded him.

"Yes, but well, I never, that is—"

Amanda came to his rescue. Stepping to her brother's side, she gave his shoulder a supportive squeeze. "I think what he's trying to say in his bumbling way, Brother Fargo, is that it might have been smarter to keep it a secret. Now Gheller is aware we're on to him and there's no predicting what he'll do."

"I get the impression he's more interested in the Mackenzies than either of you," Fargo said.

"The Mackenzies?" Amanda and Arthur repeated in unison.

Perry Hutchings, who had been listening with intense interest, interjected, "Rumor has it the mother and daughter have a hoard of gold stashed somewhere. Gold Finnian found before he was murdered. Half the men in camp have gone up into the hills trying to find their homestead, but no one has succeeded." He chortled. "A few had their hats shot off their heads, and one fellow lost part of an ear."

"Those two women are untamed catamounts," Arthur said. "I've tried to convince Marjorie to attend services, but she stubbornly refuses. The forest is her tabernacle, she says. And the only hymns she sings are in private."

"The daughter is worse," Amanda piped up. "Just last week she slapped sweet Mrs. Tilly after Mrs. Tilly suggested she stop running around in pants and wear a dress, as a proper lady should."

"It's a shame about their father," Perry Hutchings remarked. "Whoever shot him supposedly stole his poke. People say he had a nugget in it the size of a walnut, along with a lot of smaller ones."

Arthur sniffed. "Don't believe everything you hear. He showed me his big nugget once and it wasn't any larger than a grape."

"That's nothing to sneeze at," Hutchings said. "From the stories making the rounds, no one else has found any near that size."

Amanda smiled at him. "How about you? Have you found any? When you first showed up, you told us you were after gold, too."

"But you don't seem to do much prospecting," Arthur said. "From what we hear, all you do is go around asking questions."

Hutchings took a sip of water before answering. "I don't want to pick any old spot. Sure, I've been asking a lot of questions. It's the only way to narrow down a site that promises to have a high yield."

Arthur opened his mouth to say something, but Amanda poked him in the side and he closed it again.

Strolling to the cupboard, she came back with four china plates. She placed one in front of each of them and the fourth where she intended to sit.

Fargo wasn't an expert on chinaware, but he knew an expensive set when he saw it. The plates were exquisitely molded and decorated, with ripples along the outer edge and an inner ring of rainbow hues. Evidently he wasn't the only one impressed.

"These must have cost a small fortune," Perry Hutchings commented, running a finger over his. "The Laflin China Company made these, if I'm not mistaken, and they only sell the very best." He glanced at the parson. "I'm amazed a man of the cloth can afford them."

"The set was a gift from a member of our flock," Arthur said. "Not here, of course. They were given to us—"

"Somewhere else," Amanda cut in while bringing over a china bowl brimming with gravy. "The generosity of those my brother ministers to knows no bounds. Why, one time he sat at the bedside of an ailing woman for days on end. Her physician said she didn't have long to live, but she proved him wrong and recovered. To show her gratitude for what my brother had done, she gave him a gift like no other." Amanda set down the bowl and gestured at her brother. "Show them, why don't you?"

Arthur reached into an inner coat pocket and held out a watch on a long chain. Cased in gold, front and back, it also boasted a gold chain, gold fob, and fold case bow. He pried at the bezel with a fingernail and opened the front. The numbers were Roman numerals, which was customary. But where the XII and the VI should have been, small diamonds had been inset.

Fargo whistled in appreciation.

"I bet that cost more than I could earn in ten years," Hutchings said. "Don't you feel a bit guilty, Parson, accepting gifts like those?"

"Why should he?" Amanda responded. "He works hard preaching, tending the sick, helping those who can't help themselves. Is it wrong when people repay his kindness?"

"A laborer must be worthy of his hire," Arthur said.

"I try to talk them out of giving me gifts, but what am I to do when they insist?"

"I see your point," Hutchings said, but his tone implied the opposite. "Ironic, isn't it? With the china and that watch, and Lord knows what else you have hidden away, you must be the richest people in Aubrick."

"You exaggerate, sir," Arthur said. "The truth is, we barely scrape by. I've had this same coat longer than I can remember. I only have two shirts to my name, and one pair of pants. My shoes are in need of repair, my socks need stitching. Hardly the attire of someone who is excessively wealthy."

"Sell the china and that watch and you can live like kings," Hutchings suggested.

"Not for long, though," Amanda said, "and we like to take a long-term view of things. If we sell them, it won't be until we're ready for the rocking chair. The gifts we're given will see us through our waning years."

"Even parsons retire," Arthur mentioned.

Fargo didn't say anything, but he thought it odd of Amanda to take for granted she would still be living with her brother in twenty years. Most women would want to be off on their own and married, maybe even raising a family. He picked up his knife and fork and patiently waited as the rest of the meal was served; thick slabs of venison cooked to perfection, bread layered with butter, a mix of greens chopped to fine pieces and covered with a vinegary dressing, plump potatoes bursting at their skins, and to wash it down, enough coffee to fill a lake. They had salt, too, a costly condiment for most of Aubrick's population, and a bowl of sugar, an even rarer treat. Famished, he ate with relish, offering few comments. The others, though, babbled on like matrons at a sewing bee, making small talk about the camp, about the weather, about politics, and about the Indian "problem" and what should be done about it.

"How about you, Brother Fargo?" Arthur asked at that juncture. "You've had some dealings with savages, I do believe. What should be done about the Sioux and

Blackfeet and all the other tribes who persist in spilling white blood?"

Amanda had to get her say in first. "I'll tell you what *I* think should be done. They should all be exterminated. That might sound harsh, but it's the only way to stop the attacks. And I'm not the only one who feels that way."

No, she wasn't, Fargo sadly mused. Several past presidents had gone on record as saying the same. The general sentiment throughout the country was summed up in the saying, "The only good Indian is a dead Indian."

"So how about it?" the parson prodded. "How would you solve the problem?"

"I'd have all the whites move back across the Mississippi," Fargo said between chews. "Except me and maybe five or six others."

Amanda and Arthur laughed, thinking he had made a joke.

Perry Hutchings, more perceptive, lowered his spoon and said, "It's too late to stem the westward tide. The best we can hope for is that the government will set aside reserves for the Indians and then honor the commitment."

"Waste valuable land on heathens?" Amanda said.

Fargo looked at her, *really* looked at her, and felt a twinge of regret at allowing himself to be enticed by her physical charms. For underneath lay a heart as cold as high-country snow, and as merciless as a rabid wolf's. "They were here long before we were They should be entitled to their fair share."

"But life is seldom fair, is it?" This from Hutchings, who fixed a hard gaze on the Nicholsons. "I'll give you an example. Let's take a well-to-do spinster woman living in Chicago. Out of the goodness of her heart she took in her sister's children when her sister and her sister's husband died in a fire. The police believed it was deliberately set, but they never did determine who was to blame, but that's neither here nor there. It's the old woman who concerns us. She raised the children as if they were her own. She lavished love on them, put clothes on their backs, food in their bellies. Then one day she died under mysterious circumstances, too. Supposedly, she stepped out in front of a speeding carriage. But a lady who happened to be at the window of a nearby house swears the old woman was pushed by the very pair she had so lovingly raised." Hutchings paused. "Where's the fairness in that?"

The parson and Amanda, Fargo saw, had grown as still as headstones and as flinty as quartz.

"Quit beating around the bush," Amanda said, her voice devoid of all prior charm. "Come out with it plain."

"Very well," Perry Hutchings said. "The old woman was your aunt, Susan Sutton. And it was the two of you who murdered her."

6

A chill filled the room. Arthur Nicholson was a mute statue, but his sister was seething mad. Amanda reared out of her chair, her right hand drifting to the table knife beside her plate. For a moment Skye Fargo thought she was going to grab it and plunge the blade into Perry Hutchings, but she capped her temper by sheer force of will and slowly sank back down, plastering a feline grin on her features.

"So this is the thanks we get for inviting you into our humble home? You level false accusations?"

Hutchings sat back. "Spare me your mock outrage. I'm tired of all this verbal sparring. You know I've been asking questions about you. What you don't know is why, and that's the only reason you invited me tonight. To quiz me. To learn my motive."

"Why would we care?" Amanda said with deceptive innocence. "Our last name is Nicholson, not Sutton. It has nothing to do with us."

Fargo had caught her in a bald-faced lie. Not four hours ago she had mentioned an aunt named Susan who stepped in front of a speeding carriage. Coincidence? Hardly.

Amanda went blithely on. "Besides, if the old bag died two years ago, everyone has forgotten about her by now."

"Not everyone," Hutchings said. "You forget. Your mother had another sister, Agatha. She lives in Ohio, but she wrote Susan regularly, and Susan confided in her.

When Agatha heard about Susan's death she immediately suspected foul play."

Arthur found his voice. "Confided what?"

Hutchings looked at Fargo instead of the Nicholsons. "Susan was a wonderful woman. Kind, considerate, and devoutly religious. She carried a Bible with her everywhere and quoted it by the hour." He pointed at Arthur's Bible, which was on the counter. "That very Bible there. If you'll open it and look at the third page, you'll see where she scribbled her name. Someone crossed it out, but you can still read the original signature."

Fargo rose up out of his chair. Amanda made as if to grab his wrist, but she thought better of it. Sure enough, on the page indicated SUSAN DEBORAH SUTTON had been scrawled in neat, small letters. Half a dozen ink lines had been slashed across her name but it was legible nonetheless.

"Susan took these two under her wing and raised them from childhood. And how did they repay her?" Hutchings was still staring solely at Fargo, not the pair in question. "They mocked her to scorn. They drank. They smoked. They stayed out to all hours of the night. They constantly demanded money for clothes and alcohol and whatever else their selfish hearts desired. Finally, Susan Sutton had enough. She gave them an ultimatum. They had two weeks to pack their belongings and move out or she would have them forcibly evicted. Guess what they did?"

Fargo set the Bible down. Arthur was a pale sheet, but Amanda was fiery red and held herself like a panther about to pounce.

"They threatened her life," Hutchings said. "They told her that if she didn't go on giving them money and letting them do as they damn well pleased, they would kill her. On the morning she died, Susan wrote her last letter to her sister. She told Agatha of the threat, and said she had refused to give in. But she was scared. She asked Agatha to see justice done if anything happened to her."

"After Susan's death, Agatha came to Chicago and hired you," Fargo guessed.

The detective nodded. "That was almost two years ago. It's taken me all this time to track them down. They never stayed in one place more than a few months and changed their last names every time they moved." He paused. "I'm telling you all this because today I found out who you are. You're not one of Amanda's consorts, as I'd imagined."

Fargo moved to where he could see both siblings clearly. "Have you anything to say for yourselves?"

Amanda raised a hand to her throat. "Do my ears deceive me? You sound as if you actually believe him." Her glittering gaze fixed on the detective. "Let's look at your outrageous claim realistically, shall we? For the sake of argument we'll assume everything you've said is true. If the police have a witness to the alleged murder why haven't they shown up to arrest us?"

"The witness refuses to testify," Hutchings said. "She's afraid you'll kill her before the case comes to court."

Arthur broke his long silence. "How did you discover this witness?"

"By going door-to-door to every house and apartment for five blocks around," Hutchings answered. "She was willing to tell me what she saw, but she wouldn't go with me to the police no matter how I pleaded. Even Agatha couldn't persuade her."

"So there isn't a shred of evidence, is there?" Amanda said, smiling smugly. "You have nothing to link us to the old woman's death."

"Oh, I know you're the Suttons, all right," Hutchings stated. "I know your aunt had a will that left everything to you, and I know the three of you were on your way to her attorney to have it changed so you wouldn't get a cent, when you pushed her in front of the carriage. I know you sold the house and took the money and moved to New Orleans. You had enough to live in modest comfort the rest of your lives. But that wasn't enough, was it? You had to have the best clothes, the best carriage, the best china." Hutchings tapped his plate.

Amanda grew redder.

"Then there's Arthur and his gambling habit. And

your penchant for wine and men. Within seven weeks you were not only broke, you were in debt. So you left New Orleans and headed west to Kansas City. There, Arthur pretended to be a preacher and you fleeced thousands of dollars from people who could scarcely afford to part with a cent."

"Have any evidence to that effect?" Amanda asked.

Hutchings wasn't done with his account. "You had to flee Kansas City, too, when Arthur bet all you had, and more, on a horse that came in last. And you wound up here, of all places. Probably because you heard about the gold when you stopped at Fort Randall on your way to the Oregon Country."

Amanda laughed lightly. "I've heard nursery rhymes that were more entertaining."

Arthur stood. His self-confidence had reasserted itself, and he gruffly demanded, "As my sister keeps saying, where's your proof? All you have is hearsay and innuendo. Even if we are who you claim we are, there is absolutely nothing you can do to us."

It was Perry Hutchings's turn to rise. "I wouldn't be so sure. All I need do is hang around Aubrick long enough. You'll slip up. When you do, I'll be there."

Amanda pointed at the door. "I'll thank you to leave, and to keep your wild accusations to yourself."

"My flock won't like it if you slander my good name," Arthur said. "Some already want to run you off. All I need do is give the word."

"Give it, then, I defy you to." Hutchings walked wide of them, his right hand under his jacket. "I'll tell everyone just what I've told Mr. Fargo. We'll let them decide for themselves who to believe." He stopped at the door. "I mean to see you punished for your crimes. You deserve to hang, but I'll settle for putting you both behind bars."

"Get out!" Arthur commanded. "And don't dare step foot over our threshold again!"

For half a minute after the door closed no one uttered a word. Amanda broke the silence by saying, "Please tell me I'm wrong, Skye. Please tell me you don't believe his vicious lies. Not after— " She coyly bowed her chin.

Fargo let his actions speak for him. Moving to the corner, he commenced to gather up his belongings.

Amanda was dumbfounded but not for long. "Think about what you're doing. If you walk out, it will be the same as slapping us in the face. You're taking his side against ours, and you haven't even heard us out."

"I don't need to." Fargo draped his saddle blanket, saddlebags, and the bridle over his left shoulder. Holding the saddle in his left hand, low at his side, he gripped the Henry with his other.

Amanda refused to give up. "You don't know what you'll be missing," she said, striking a seductive pose.

"Yes, I do." Fargo was careful not to pass too close to her and her table knife. Pushing the door wide, he walked toward the Ovaro. Brother and sister watched him saddle up and adjust the bridle.

"Mark my words," Amanda said as he stepped into the stirrups. "If you ride off, you can consider us bitter enemies."

Touching a finger to his hat brim, Fargo applied his spurs. He rode south to the road to give the false impression he was heading off down the valley, but once he was out of sight he swung eastward to the base of the hills and then northward until he came to the gully. He paralleled it to the tree line, went a short distance into the woods, and drew rein in a clearing. Dismounting, he stripped the pinto and made a cold camp. It would be too conspicuous to have a fire so he did without. With the saddle for a pillow, he stretched out on his back, pulled his blanket to his chin, and admired the celestial spectacle until sleep claimed him.

As was his habit, Fargo awoke shortly before daybreak. He rolled up his bedroll, treated himself to a piece of pemmican for breakfast, and by the time a golden crown emblazoned the rim of the world, he was in the saddle. He had no trouble finding the spot where Bethany had entered the trees, and a few minutes of searching rewarded him with a heel print. A few yards more and he saw crushed grass and a broken twig. She had been running, and her trail was plain enough to enable him to follow it without having to climb down.

A crisp morning chill clung to the woodland. Birds chirped and squawked. Squirrels greeted the new day with irate chattering, as if they were mad at having their rest disturbed. A doe and fawn, startled from a thicket, flitted off through the boles. A little later a rabbit bounded out from under the stallion's very hooves.

Fargo was in no particular hurry. If it took all day to find the Mackenzies, it wouldn't bother him in the least. His sole intent was to talk to them—and see Bethany again.

The tracks took him up over the hill. From the crest Fargo had a sweeping view of the entire valley. Prospectors were moving north along the stream to their diggings to begin another backbreaking day of toil and sweat. People were moving about in Aubrick, but in Lodestone hardly a soul yet stirred. Which figured. Lodestone's inhabitants were accustomed to staying up until all hours of the night and sleeping in until noon, a luxury the hardworking folks in Aubrick could ill afford. He saw no sign of activity at the church.

Midway down the opposite slope, the tracks revealed Bethany had caught up with her mother. From there the two hiked side-by-side. Oddly, they'd made no attempt to conceal their footprints, which puzzled Fargo since others had tried to track them down and failed. At the bottom they had turned north, winding along a game trail frequently used by elk, deer, and bears. A clever trick, sufficient to throw off inexperienced trackers, but not someone as skilled as Fargo.

After half a mile the vegetation thinned. The soil became rockier. The Mackenzies had left the game trail, bearing northwest, and from then on they did their utmost to conceal their sign.

Fargo had to hand it to them. They were devious. They stuck to the stoniest ground. They avoided bare earth and random tracts of short-stemmed grass. To stay on their trail he had to climb down and lead the Ovaro by the reins so he could study the ground closely. It was slow going. Complete footprints were few and exceedingly far between. The most he found were occasional smudges and two or three partial tracks. Often, he covered twenty or thirty yards without finding anything before the outline of a sole or the indentation of a heel would verify that he hadn't lost them.

By late in the morning Fargo was roving amid the gorges and cliffs that pockmarked the north end of the valley. The tracks brought him to a craggy height overlooking the stream. Far below, prospectors were working their claims. Some were panning. Some were busy at their sluices. Others were relying on picks and chisels. Engrossed in their work, they didn't spot him, and soon he was beyond the escarpment and moving across a bluff banked hot by the sun. Here the ground was solid rock and there were no footprints at all; no smudges, no heel marks, nothing.

Fargo continued along the bluff in the direction the women had been heading for another two hundred yards, until he was forced to stop. The trail had buckled up ahead, leaving a steep but negotiable slope littered with loose rocks, mosses, and earth. Judging from the vegetation, Fargo guessed the source to be a geologic cataclysm that took place ages ago. Clearly imprinted a few feet down was the sole of Bethany's left shoe. The women had wound along a ribbon of solid stone that twisted from top to bottom like the serpentine coils of a huge snake. He would have no problem descending, but the stallion was another matter. The footing was treacherous for a horse, and he refused to put the pinto at undue risk. There had to be another way down.

Roving along the bluff's edge, Fargo discovered it bordered a hidden canyon. A cliff was to the west. To the north lay a largely barren hill. Vegetation thrived on the canyon floor thanks to a spring, a pristine pocket of verdant growth in the midst of rocky desolation. An ideal spot, he thought, for the Mackenzies' homestead. Yet although he scoured the canyon from end to end he saw no indication of human habitation, not a cabin nor a lean-to nor even a tent.

Presently, Fargo found another way down, a dry wash that separated the bluff from the hill. Reaching it was a challenge since he had to navigate a switchback barely wide enough for the Ovaro, but once there, the wash afforded rapid access to the canyon. As they neared the bottom he forked leather and reached for the Henry. He started to shuck it from the scabbard but released his hold. If he rode in with the rifle out, the Mackenzies might surmise he meant to do them harm, and he didn't want that.

At a walk Fargo rode into a stand of saplings. Lush grass and clusters of wildflowers carpeted the ground, muffling the pinto's hoofbeats. A finch warbled at him from a nearby low limb. A butterfly flitted on gossamer wings. Since tracks were most likely to be found near the spring, that was where he headed. Scarcely a dozen yards farther, low voices reached him, borne by a stiff wind out of the west from the vicinity of the high cliff. Taking a gamble he rode toward it, out in the open to demonstrate his intentions were peaceful.

A dark spot at the base of the cliff caught Fargo's eye. It appeared to be a large shadow, but as he grew closer he saw a wide opening. Not to a cave, but a grotto, an erosion-worn pocket nine feet high and twice that in length. In the center crackled a fire. The smoke was dissipated by the breeze long before it wafted up out of the canyon. A small animal was roasting on a makeshift spit. A rabbit, going by the shape and size. A log table, log chairs, and not one but two log beds were added proof he had found what he was after.

Of the Mackenzies, though, there was no trace.

Twenty feet out from the opening, Fargo heard the metallic rasp of a rifle hammer being curled back. Shifting to his right, he beheld Marjorie Mackenzie with her Sharps trained on his torso.

"That'll be far enough, mister."

To his left another hammer clicked. Bethany had him

in the sights of her Spencer. "Raise your hands and keep them raised."

Fargo did as he was bid. "Pleased to see you again, ladies," he said, smiling. "Looks like I'm just in time for dinner."

Mother and daughter advanced from either side, as wary as cougars who had cornered a bear. "How the blazes did you find us?" Marjorie demanded. "No one else has been able to, and some were mighty good at trackin'."

"Not good enough," Fargo said, casually raising his left leg and hooking it over his saddle horn. "I'm one of the best there is at what I do." He wasn't bragging. It was plain and simple fact. His early days with the Sioux, his life in the wilderness, had honed his woodlore to a degree few rivaled.

"Listen to him, Ma!" Bethany declared. "Next he'll be tellin' us he can walk on water."

"No, but I can drink it," Fargo said. "And I wouldn't mind wetting my throat right about now." He nodded at the grotto. "Mind if I climb down and join you?"

His politeness perplexed them. Marjorie sidled around to the front of the stallion, her features scrunched in indecision. "I don't know what to make of you, mister. You're not like those curly wolves down to Lodestone." A suggestion of a grin touched her mouth. "Were I forty years younger, that smile of yours would charm the britches right off me."

'Ma!" Bethany exclaimed, appalled.

"I'm joshin', girl. Don't get in a snit."

"I say we run him off," Bethany said. "And if he ever has the gall to come back, we put a few windows in his skull. This is our claim, and ours alone, and no one else is welcome."

Marjorie took her right hand off the sharps to scratch her chin, pondering. "The problem is, girl, he knows about this place now. If we run him off, what's to stop him from coming back with a lot of others to run *us* off? The way I see it, we've got no choice but to trust him."

"There's one other choice." Bethany circled to her

mothers' side. "We can shoot him, and our secret will be safe."

"In cold blood?" Marjorie clucked like an irritated hen. "Is that the best your pa and me learned you, girl? To murder people like your pa was murdered? To stoop to being as low-down as the bastard who did it?"

"But, Ma—" Bethany tried to interrupt.

"Hush when I'm talkin'. Your pa and me might not have amounted to much as this world goes, but we always tried to rear your decent. We taught you to have respect for others, and only show your claws when they do the same."

Fargo was being ignored. Lowering his left leg, he swung down and let the reins dangle. Bethany tensed, thrusting the Spencer's muzzle at his face, but he strolled by her without a sideways glance. "While the two of you hash it out, I'll help myself to some of that rabbit." He could feel Bethany's eyes bore into his back and for a few anxious seconds he thought she really would fire. But he reached the grotto in one piece, and hunkering, pried at the meat with his fingers. A hot, greasy chunk came off in his palm and he took a bite. "Mmm. Not bad. My compliments to the cook."

"We didn't say you could eat our food," Bethany protested. They had entered on his heels, and she was still covering him with her rifle.

Her mother, though, had lowered the Sharps, more amused than anything else. "What are you after, mister? Why did you go to all the trouble to find us?"

"It should be obvious, Ma," Bethany said. "This polecat has a hankerin' for the gold he thinks we have. He's heard all the rumors and figures to get rich at our expense." She glared hot coals. "But that's all they are. Rumors."

"That isn't what you told Riley and Kenny yesterday," Fargo mentioned, his mouth full of juicy meat.

Mother and daughter started as if pricked with pins. "What's he talking about?" Marjorie asked. "What did you tell those two?"

"Nothing, Ma. Honest," Bethany responded. "How would this fella know what was said, anyhow?"

"I was there," Fargo revealed. "I saw them follow your mother out of Lodestone, and I was about to stop them when you popped up. Kenny offered you thirty dollars, remember? For directions to your homestead? And you told him," Fargo quoted her exactly. " 'We don't need no paltry thirty dollars. We have plenty of go—' " Smacking his lips, he helped himself to another piece of rabbit. "You never finished what you were saying, but you didn't have to. I saw their faces."

"You *were* there!" Bethany bleated.

"Oh Lord," Marjorie said. "Those two must have gone back and blabbed to everyone they saw. We'll have more greedy polecats than ever out lookin' for us."

"Maybe not," Fargo said. "If they told anyone it was Slan Gheller. And Gheller would keep it to himself."

Marjorie arched an eyebrow. "Why? To protect us? Are you sayin' he's not the worthless cur I've pegged him as? He keeps sayin' all he's interested in is Beth, but if you ask me, he's lyin' through his teeth."

"You saw his saloon yesterday. Why should he care about your gold when he can get everyone else's? The prospectors are spending what they find as fast as they find it. Another six months to a year and Gheller will be one of the two wealthiest men in the valley."

"Who's the other?"

"Arthur Nicholson." Fargo almost said "Sutton."

"The parson?" Marjorie laughed. "Is he out prospectin' along with all the rest? A man of the cloth should know better."

Bethany had something else on her mind. "How about you, mister? You still haven't told us what you're doing here. If you're not out for the gold, then what?"

Fargo looked her up and down, from her luxurious hair to her shapely calves, and she blushed. "Things are about to heat up in the valley, and the two of you could get caught up in the middle."

"What do you know that we don't?" Marjorie queried.

"Only that a lot more blood promises to be shed and

I don't want any of it to be yours or you daughter's."
Fargo was intentionally vague because he doubted they
would believe the truth. Few would. Arthur and Amanda
were too widely respected. True, Marjorie wasn't a
churchgoer, but it wouldn't strengthen her confidence in
him if he made wild allegations.

"Why should you care what happens to us?" Bethany
asked. "You don't know us from Eve."

"I don't like being used. Someone tried to arrange
things so I'd kill Gheller or he'd kill me. I'm out to pay
them back. And if I'm not mistaken, the same people
are to blame for Finnian's death. By helping you, I
help myself."

Bristling like a porcupine, Marjorie took a step. "You
know who murdered my Fin? Tell me who they are! I'll
bed them down permanent."

"I don't want to say until I have more proof," Fargo
said. Without it, no one would believe him. Small wonder
Perry Hutchings hadn't told anyone, either.

"So all we have to go on is your say-so?" Bethany
snickered. "I'd sooner trust a politician."

Marjorie moved around the fire and roosted on a flat
boulder put there for that express purpose. "I'm a heap
older than you are, girl, and I know a lot more about
human nature. I say we hear this gent out before we
rush to judgment."

Fargo grinned. This from the woman who was ready
to scatter his brains all over the saloon a day ago.

"What's your plan?"

"I don't have one," Fargo confessed.

Bethany chortled. "And you want us to partner up
with you? Why should we? What can you do that we
can't accomplish on our own?"

"I might be able to flush out your father's killer."
Fargo had been contemplating all morning how best to
expose Arthur and Amanda for the ruthless killers they
were, and he had a few promising ideas.

"We're listening, mister," Marjorie said.

"After dinner." Fargo bit into the rabbit. "I don't like
to do a lot of talking on an empty stomach."

77

Bethany removed her hat and gave her head a toss. Waves of curly hair cascaded over her slender shoulders, framing a face as near-perfect as Nature ever devised. Drawing a knife, she hacked off a piece for herself and held it daintily in both hands.

Marjorie dispensed with etiquette. Using her nails, she tore off a leg and tore into it like a famished she-wolf.

Fargo idly scanned the grotto. "No wonder no one could find your cabin. You don't have one." A gleam caught his eye, and he gawked, bedazzled by sparkling veins of glittering ore that laced the rear wall and part of the ceiling. Veins five to six inches wide, and solid yellow. "It can't be!" he blurted.

Marjorie smiled. "So now you know our secret. You're sittin' across from two of the richest women in the world."

7

Marjorie Mackenzie hadn't exaggerated. The veins lining the grotto wall and ceiling were solid gold ore, the purest and rarest form. Gold that would take years to extract. Millions of dollars' worth, maybe hundreds of millions. A once-in-a-lifetime strike, the kind that was every prospector's dream come true.

"The funny thing is," Marjorie said as Fargo ran a hand over a yellow vein on the rear wall "we didn't come to this valley lookin' to get rich. Fin and me were fixin' to start a farm. The soil is rich and there's water for irrigation. But we'd hardly started to look around when he spotted a Sioux war party. They were just passin' through and had no idea we were here, but we didn't take no chances. We hightailed it to the north end of the valley to hide out until they were long gone. It was a sheer fluke we stumbled onto this canyon. Fin liked to say Providence had a hand, but if that's the case, I'd rather the Good Lord had left me Fin instead of all this gold."

"I was the one who found the ore," Bethany related. "We were camped by the spring. I got restless, so I took a torch and was pokin' around when I saw a flash of yellow."

"My Fin couldn't believe it at first," Marjorie said, laughing. "He thought it had to be fool's gold. He kept pinchin' himself and sayin', 'I must be drunk.'"

Fargo might have done the same. His right boot brushed something that rolled under his sole, and he looked down to find pieces of ore, of varying size, that had been chipped loose. Three picks were propped against the wall. To his left, saddlebags and large deer-hide pouches had been piled, crammed with gold. The Mackenzies had been busy.

"We plan to work another three or four months and gather up a ton," Marjorie related. "Then we'll buy us a wagon and sneak off to one of the settlements to deposit all we have in a bank. Rutledge, maybe. I hear they've got a fine one."

"We've been mighty worried about havin' our find stole out from under us," Bethany mentioned. "Our claim isn't exactly legal. No one's is. The nearest assayer's office is clear off in Denver, and we can't afford to take two weeks off to travel there and back." She paused. "The parson has been makin' a list of claims, which everyone is beholden to honor. But we haven't told him where our strike is."

"I should say not!" Marjorie declared. "A find this size, every greedy weasel in the valley will want to get their hands on it! We'd be bushwhacked, sure as shootin', just like my sweet Fin."

Fargo squatted and examined a piece of ore the size of his fist. "Where was your husband when he was shot?"

"About a quarter of a mile south of here," Marjorie said. "He was on his way back from Aubrick. We found some tracks, where someone had come runnin' up behind him. Near as we could tell, the two of them talked a spell, then Fin turned to go. That's when the bastard shot him."

"It had to be someone he knew," Bethany said. "My pa was too savvy to turn his back to a stranger."

"Slan Gheller," Marjorie said. "Had to be. He was always pesterin' us about our strike. Always sneakin' around tryin' to find it." Her face softened. "My poor Fin. Done in like that. He crawled thirty yards from where he was shot, tryin' to reach us, to reach me." Her eyes glistened wetly. "I miss him so damn much. I'd always hoped I'd be the one to go first 'cause I knew it would tear me up inside. The nights are the worst. Lyin' there all alone, rememberin' how much—"

"Don't, Ma." Bethany went to her mother and draped an arm across Marjorie's shoulders. "Don't pain yourself so."

"I can't help it, girl." Sniffling, Marjorie dabbed at her eyes with a sleeve. "I loved him so. Your pa was the finest man I ever met. He always treated me decent. Always did his best to give me the life I wanted. We had us some grand times over the years. No one could make me smile like Fin."

Fargo returned to the fire carrying the large piece of ore. Bethany, he observed, had the Spencer by her side, and placed a hand on it, as distrustful as ever.

"Thinkin' of helpin' yourself?" she said resentfully. "I bet you've never seen so much pure gold in all your born days."

"You might win the bet," Fargo said. "As for this," he wagged the ore, "I don't want it for myself. I was thinking of using it as bait to catch the person who shot your father."

Bethany cocked an eye. "Are you addlepated? How can you not be interested in *gold*? Most men would have plugged us the moment they saw our strike."

"I don't have any interest in being rich." Fargo sat and held the ore close to the flames. It had to weigh two pounds or more.

"Do you hear him, Ma?" Bethany said. "What more proof do you need he's a born liar? There isn't a man alive who wouldn't give his eyeteeth to be as wealthy as King Midas."

Dropping the ore at his feet, Fargo leaned back. "Tell me something. What are you going to do with all your riches?"

"What most folks do. Buy us a mansion back East, with servants and a fancy carriage and all the trimmings. Get us a bunch of pretty dresses and go to balls and the theater." Bethany glowed with her heart's desire. "We'll live like true ladies. We'll have a maid to do the cleanin' and a cook to do the cookin' and one of those butlers to answer the door when somebody comes callin'. Handsome fellas will fall all over themselves askin' me out."

She sighed dreamily. "It will be heaven. All I've ever wanted out of life."

"It's all most people want," Fargo conceded. "But I'm not ready to settle down yet. I like to travel, to see what's over the next ridge. I own a good horse, a rifle and a pistol, and the clothes on my back, and that's all I need right now. Even if I was as rich as Midas, it wouldn't change things. I'd still go on living the way I am."

"You're a strange coon," Bethany said.

Marjorie stirred. "No, he's not. He's got more sense than most. He doesn't crave money above all else. He doesn't have our weakness."

"Oh, I have a weakness." Fargo deliberately ogled Bethany again, and she blushed more beautifully than before. "So now you know why I don't have any interest in your gold. That, and one other reason. The most important of all."

"What would that be?" Bethany asked.

"By rights it's yours, and yours alone. You found it. You're entitled to it."

Bethany shook her head in confusion. "You're a bewilderment, mister. You're either the most honest man I've ever met, or the biggest jackass. I can't decide which."

Marjorie pointed at the ore. "Do you really reckon it will help?"

"If we play our cards right," Fargo said. "Whoever did it is greedy enough to kill. If I feed their greed they might try again."

"But you'll be their target," Bethany said, peering intently at him. "You'll be puttin' your life at risk on our account."

Rising, Marjorie walked to the pile of saddlebags and leather pouches and brought over a pair of the former bulging at the seams. "As my grandpa used to say, the bigger the bait, the bigger the fish. Take this, and more besides if it'll help."

Fargo opened one of the flaps. The saddlebags contained enough gold to nestle a person in the lap of luxury for years. "This should be more than enough."

"When do you aim to put your plan into effect?" Marjorie inquired.

"As soon as I'm done eating." Fargo estimated it would take him an hour and a half to reach the camps by taking a more direct route and holding to a trot most of the way.

"What's your rush?" Marjorie smiled. "Lodestone gets liveliest after the sun goes down. Wait until then. You're welcome to spend the afternoon with us. We never have anyone to jaw with except ourselves."

Bethany still wasn't pacified. "I swear, Ma. What's gotten into you? The only other man you've ever treated this nicely was pa."

"It's his eyes, girl." Marjorie resumed gnawing on the rabbit leg. "Folks say the eyes are the window to the soul, and I believe 'em. Your pa had the kindest, nicest eyes, except when he was riled. Slan Gheller has the eyes of a snake. Cass Benedict—well, I'm not too sure about him. I hear he's a killer, but his eyes say otherwise."

"And Fargo?" Bethany prompted.

Marjorie gazed across at him. "His remind me of the prairie on a warm summer's day. Or the mountains in the spring, when the grass has turned green and new leaves are on the trees."

"*This* jasper's eyes? They don't look no different than any other fella's to me. Bluer, maybe, but that's all."

Marjorie cupped a hand to her mouth and pretended to say confidentially, "You'll have to forgive her. She's young yet, and hasn't had much to do with people. Think of her as a mustang that ain't never been broke."

"Ma!" Bethany protested.

The older woman was in a talkative mood, and for the next half hour related her life's story. How she had been raised in a small town in northern Kentucky. How Finnian had swept her off her feet, and the two of them had done what everyone else was doing and gone west to carve out a new life. They got as far as Missouri, and used all the money they had scrimped and saved as a down payment on a modest farm. Until about a year ago

83

all had gone well, and they'd enjoyed a happy life together.

"Or as happy as this life gets. But we always lived hand-to-mouth. There was never much extra money after we sold our crops. What little there was we put back into the farm, buying stock and equipment and such."

Bethany took up the tale when her mother stopped. "Then last summer things took a turn for the worse. Missouri had its worst dry spell in as long as anyone could remember. There was no rain for months on end. Crops withered. Poultry dropped like flies. So did cattle. Hundreds of farmers lost their farms."

Not all that long ago Fargo had guided a wagon train through the Rockies to the Great Salt Lake. It had been made up mainly of displaced farmers, all of whom had their own tale of woe to share.

"We were one of them," Marjorie said. "My Fin tried his best. We put out towels to soak up the mornin' dew. We paid out the last of our money for a water witch. Three times the divinin' rod showed us where water should be. Three times we dug down a hundred feet or better, but the holes always came up dry." She glumly stopped chewing. "We were at our wit's end. Our mortgage was long overdue. Creditors were demandin' money we didn't have. So we sold off all we had left, settled our debts as best we were able, and lit out for Oregon."

Bethany gazed off into the distance. "The land of milk and honey, they call it. Where it rains six months of the year and the earth is fertile. Where land is cheap, and most of the Indians are friendly."

"It sounded like paradise," Marjorie said. "But we never got there. When Fin saw how nice this country was, he talked me into settlin' here instead. I wish to God I'd never given in. If I hadn't he'd still be alive."

"No one can predict the future," Fargo said kindly.

Marjorie hung her head low. "Maybe not. But I had me a strong feelin'. A feelin' we should keep going. But to please Fin I agreed to stay. Until the day I die, I will never forgive myself for that. Not ever."

"Don't be so hard on yourself, Ma," Bethany sought

to cheer her. "You did it because you loved him. How can it be wrong if you did it out of love?"

A groan escaped Marjorie. Slowing rising, she walked from the grotto, never once raising her head. A portrait of despair, she shuffled off through the trees.

"I should go after her," Bethany said, standing.

"She probably wants to be alone," Fargo advised. He helped himself to a third handful of rabbit and lay on his side, his head propped in his free hand. "Give her half an hour and she'll be herself again."

Bethany took a step away, then stopped, racked by indecision. "It's been awful hard on her since pa's death. Sometimes she acts as if all the life is drained out of her. That if it weren't for me, she'd gladly climb to the top of the cliff and throw herself off so she could be with him again."

"When this is over take her on a tour of the East, or maybe Europe. It'll take her mind off Fin." Fargo bit down on a juicy morsel of fat. "You'll have enough money to go wherever you want, do whatever you feel like doing."

"So now you're an expert on human nature?"

Fargo answered her question with one of his own. "Are you part mule by any chance? Every time I open my mouth, you kick me in the teeth." He chuckled. "If I didn't know any better I'd swear we were married."

"The day I'd hitch myself to the likes of you is the day cows sprout wings and fly," Bethany jousted. "You're not my type."

"Saving yourself for a handsome prince?" Fargo liked how her nostrils flared when she was angry. "Just remember. Save yourself too long and you'll wind up a spinster, with a cat for company."

"I seriously think I hate you," Bethany said, and flounced out, so agitated she left the Spencer behind. Her bottom swayed enticingly with every stomp of her foot. The first pine she came to, she kicked and spat, "Men!" Slanting toward the spring, she soon blended into the vegetation.

Fargo liked women with spunk. More the better when

they were young and alluring. He filled his belly, then rested his cheek on his forearm. It promised to be a long night so a nap was in order. He didn't expect to sleep much more than an hour, but when he opened his eyes again the shadows had lengthened into late afternoon.

Across the fire sat Marjorie. She had been watching him as he slept. "I have one thing to ask of you, Mr. Fargo."

"Ma'am?"

"Treat her nice. I'm smart enough to realize you're not the marryin' kind so I won't ask more than that."

Sluggish from his rest, Fargo sat up. "You can't be talking about what I think you're talking about."

"Posh. That's the first stupid thing you've said since we met. I'm old, but I'm not senile. My girl has taken a shine to you and I want you to be gentle. She's not experienced in worldly ways."

Fargo stretched, and rose. "If your daughter likes me, she has an unusual way of showing affection."

"When a woman pushes a man away, sometimes it's the same as grabbin' him close. I was her age once. We put on airs and act high and mighty, but some feelin's are too strong to be denied."

The subject of their discussion picked that moment to return. Bethany's arms were folded across her chest and she was sulking. "I reckon we should head out soon. It'll be dark in a couple of hours."

"We?" Fargo asked.

The raven-tressed lovely walked straight to her rifle. "If you think I'm lettin' you out of my sight with all that gold, you have another thing comin'. What's to stop you from takin' it and ridin' clear on out of the valley?"

"He wouldn't steal from us, girl," Marjorie came to his defense. "You've got to learn to trust your instincts."

"I'm not as smitten by him as you are, Ma. To earn my trust he has to do it the hard way. He has to prove he's worthy." Bethany's strawberry lips curled in a taunting challenge. "Reckon you can do that, Mr. Know-it-all?"

"Only one way to find out." Snagging the saddlebags,

Fargo slung them over a shoulder and nodded at Marjorie. "I'll bring it all back. Wait and see."

"To hell with the gold. Just bring back my daughter. She's all I really care about." Marjorie surprised him by giving him a quick hug. "As for you, young lady, I won't waste my breath tryin' to talk you out of going. You're as hardheaded as me once you put your mind to something. But you watch yourself, hear? Losin' one family member in a lifetime is more than anyone should have to bear."

"Don't fret none about me, Ma. I can shoot as straight as any man."

The sun was well on its westward descent. Fargo tied the gold-filled saddlebags behind his own and led the Ovaro to the spring. While the stallion drank, he slaked his own thirst. Bethany stood back a few yards, as cautious as a kitten. When he mounted and extended a hand, she looked at him as if he were holding out a bouquet of thorns.

"What's that for?"

"We're riding double. Unless you plan to walk the entire way."

"The two of us on the same horse?" Bethany didn't like it one bit. "I'd rather jump naked into a bed of cactus."

"There would be a sight worth seeing," Fargo quipped.

"Keep it up and I'm liable to use your eyeballs for target practice," Bethany threatened. After a few moments of indecision she reluctantly clasped his wrist and permitted him to swing her up behind him. Placing the Spencer between them, across her legs, she rested a hand on his shoulder. "Let's go."

"Better hold on tighter than that," Fargo said, raising the reins. "I wouldn't want you to fall off."

"Don't worry about me. Just because we don't own a horse doesn't mean I can't ride." Bethany poked him. "So light a shuck. And try not to ride into any trees."

Fargo jabbed his spurs a little harder than he needed to, and the stallion sprang forward as if fired from a cannon. Bethany lurched backward. Instinctively, she wrapped an arm around his waist to keep from being thrown. Her face brushed the nape of his neck, and he felt her warm breath on his skin. "That's better," he said.

"You did that on purpose, damn you."

Fargo reined toward the dry wash. The switchback above it promised to pose a challenge, but by dismounting and leading the pinto they should gain the bluff without too much difficulty.

"What in Sam hill do you think you're doing?" Bethany demanded.

"Going out the way I came in."

"By the wash? There's another way, a shorter way. We take it when we go into Aubrick. But we always come back by the long route to make it harder for polecats like Gheller to follow us." Bethany pointed at the south end of the canyon, which was deep in shadow. By accident, or design, her hand brushed his ear. "Head there."

A short ride brought them to where the bluff and the cliff molded into a seemingly impassable rock barrier thirty feet high. Fargo looked for an opening but saw none. The closer they grew, the deeper the shadows. When they were a stone's throw away and he was about to draw rein, Bethany tapped his shoulder.

"Bear a little to the left."

Slowing, Fargo obliged. He was about to remark that he still didn't see a way out when a dark vertical band hinted more was there than met the eye. The wall was cracked, a five-foot-wide split, possibly caused by the same geologic upheaval that had collapsed part of the east bluff. Cool air washed over him as he entered. The opening was barely wide enough for a horse and the stallion nickered, not liking the cramped confines. A premature twilight shrouded them.

"Be ready to stop when I say so," Bethany directed.

Over a dozen sharp twists and turns had to be negotiated. About the time a seemingly solid wall towered ahead, Bethany told him to halt, and Fargo reined up. She slid off and cat-footed around a hidden bend. For over a minute Fargo sat in the gloom, waiting, until she called out.

"The coast is clear. Come on through."

The secret cleft brought them out a hundred yards east of the stream. Gigantic slabs of rock lay in front, effectively hiding the opening from prying eyes. How the Mackenzies had initially found it, Fargo couldn't begin to imagine.

As if Bethany were reading his thoughts, she idly commented, "If not for Ma, we'd never have known that was there. She was the one who noticed it after Pa brought us in among the rocks to hide from the Sioux."

Fargo rose in the stirrups to confirm no one else was anywhere around. Bending, he grabbed her forearm, and this time she swung up without complaint.

"Only one prospector works this section of the stream," Bethany mentioned as they moved into the open, "but he's been spendin' most of his time in Lodestone of late."

Fargo wondered where the gold in the stream came from. True, the stream flowed past the cliff that flanked the hidden canyon to the west, but at no point did it come anywhere near the grotto. There had to be another source. Maybe the grotto wasn't the mother lode after all. Maybe the veins were just part of it, and there was a lot more gold under the ground.

"What is it about you my ma likes so much?" Bethany unexpectedly asked. "I've never seen her take a shine to a fella like she has to you."

"She's a good judge of character," Fargo said, grinning.

"You'd like me to believe that, wouldn't you? But I still say there's more to you than meets the eye. You're after something. I just haven't figured out what it is yet."

"You keep thinking," Fargo said. "Maybe it will come to you." To help her, he leaned back so his shoulder blades pressed against her chest. For a few tantalizing seconds he felt her breasts against his body. Then she pulled away.

The lower third of the sun had been devoured by the

horizon. Since Fargo would rather arrive in Lodestone well after dark, he held to a walk. Bethany hardly said three words until they rounded a bend and the lights of the two camps came into view.

"We're almost there. Remember, where you go, I go."

"You can't come into the saloon," Fargo flatly set her straight.

"Like hell I can't. I can take care of myself. Any man who so much as looks at me crosswise will regret it."

Fargo brought the Ovaro to a halt and swiveled in the saddle. "Let's get something straight. We do this my way, or you can hop on down, take the gold back to your mother, and tell her you were too pigheaded to do what you should."

"Pigheaded? *Me*?" Bethany was indignant.

"The people we're after aren't stupid. If we walk into the saloon together they'll know we're up to something. You're waiting outside whether you like it or not."

"You have some nerve, mister. If it weren't for ma I'd tell you to go to hell. But she has high hopes you can ferret out pa's killer and I'd hate to disappoint her after all she's been through."

Fargo faced around and clucked to the pinto. To appease her, he said, "If it will make you feel any better, you can hold onto my horse while I'm in Gheller's place. As a guarantee I won't run off."

"With the gold you have, you could buy a hundred horses."

"Not like this one." Fargo gave the Ovaro several affectionate pats. "I care for this stallion more than I do most people I meet."

Bethany was offended. "Does that include me?"

"I'd like you a lot more if you nagged me a lot less," Fargo answered. "So what's it going to be? Either you agree to do as I say or we call it off."

Her response was spat through clenched teeth. "I agree. But if you're not on the level, Gheller and his gunnies will be the least of your worries. I'll kill you my own self. So help me God."

8

Skye Fargo ambled into the Aces High with the gold-filled saddlebags over his left shoulder and paused just inside the batwing doors. On his last visit he thought the place had been packed, but that was nothing compared to now. Patrons crammed every square foot of available space. They were lined up four deep at the bar, three deep along the walls. They thronged each table, blocking off the aisles. Virtually every prospector in the valley was there, along with the ever-winsome and ever-willing doves in their tight dresses, each an oasis of color in a sea of drab and dirty homespun.

The din was enough to raise the rafters. Bellows, curses, and laughter punctuated a constant hubbub of voices. So did the clink of glasses and the rattle of the roulette wheel. The smell of liquor was strong, the reek of cigar and cigarette smoke even stronger. Everyone was having a grand old time.

Slan Gheller was at his private table, playing cards with three other men. Behind him, arrayed from left to right, were Riley, Kenny, and Cass Benedict. The short gunman was leaning against the wall, oozing boredom, but his attitude changed when Fargo barreled through a knot of onlookers and plunked the saddlebags down on the table with a loud *thump*. Straightening, Benedict lowered his right hand to the butt of his ivory-handled Colt.

Slan Gheller, involved in shuffling the deck, glanced up in surprise. "Well, look what the cat dragged in. I figured the parson and his sister would keep you on a tight leash from here on out. Or have they been filling your ears with more lies about me?"

"I take it you haven't heard," Fargo said. "The Nicholsons and I have parted company. I'm on my own now."

Gheller laughed heartily. "I'd have given a thousand dollars to see Amanda's face when you walked out. She doesn't take kindly to being bucked. Trust me. I know." He eyed the bulging saddlebags. "What's in there? Your dirty laundry?"

"I'd like to sit in on your game if you have an opening," Fargo said.

"There's always room for one more." Gheller flicked a finger at Riley, who walked over to another table, tapped a prospector on the shoulder, and motioned for the man to vacate his chair. The prospector looked over at Gheller, and did so, smiling broadly.

"Here you go, boss," Riley said, sliding in next to his employers.

Out of curiosity, many watched to see what developed. He pushed his hat back, made a teepee of his hands, and smiled at Lodestone's founder. "You lied to me, Slan." Before Gheller could take offense, he said, "You and everyone else. They had me believing the Mackenzies struck the mother lode."

"That's the rumor, mister," another player said. "Those gals have a fortune in ore hid up in the hills somewhere."

"If they do it's not from the mother lode," Fargo said.

"How would you know, stranger?" a third man scoffed. "Did you ask real nice-like and they fessed up?"

"No," Fargo said. Undoing the flaps, he raised the saddlebags over the middle of the table. "Because I found the mother lode myself." He upended them, and out spilled the gold ore, a rain of glittering golden rocks, some huge, some small, the majority the size of apples. They formed a sparkling pile a foot high.

Those at the table were too astounded to move or speak. Not so those around it, who nudged people next to them, whispered excitedly, and pointed. Men stopped whatever they were doing to turn and gape. Card games came to an abrupt stop. Dice and roulette wheels were neglected. All conversation ceased. It became so quiet that Fargo could hear a player across the table suck in a deep breath.

"God in heaven!"

"Solid gold!" a second marveled.

A third, over by the bar, hollered, "Land sakes, friend! You've done what all of us are hoping to do. You've struck it rich!"

Slan Gheller made bold to heft one of the larger pieces. "This is bigger than a goose egg. Must weight a pound or more." Grinning, he winked at Fargo. "What do you say? Care to buy a third interest in the Aces High?"

"What do I need with a saloon when there's a hundred times as much ore where this came from?" Fargo, and his gold, were the sole object of attention of everyone present. Envy was mirrored on many a face, envy mixed with large dollops of raw greed. A few fingered guns or knives but none dared use them. Not there, at any event.

"I don't suppose you'd be willin' to tell us where you found it?" asked a graybeard in shabbier clothes than most. He cackled to show he was joking and others joined in, but their laughter was hollow. Deep down they all wanted to know the same thing.

"Afraid not," Fargo said. Having made the impression he wanted, he began shoving the ore back into the saddlebags. The prospectors were riveted to every movement, many wearing frowns that lengthened as each piece of gold disappeared. When all but the larger piece in Slan Gheller's hand had been replaced, Fargo turned to him and said, "I need chips for the game. How much are you willing to offer?"

"My standard policy is three-fourths of the value. For a nugget worth, say, twenty dollars, I'll extend fifteen dollars in chips." Gheller went to rise. "I have a scale behind the bar. We'll weight this one and see how much it's worth."

"Three-fourths? Is that all?" Shaking his head, Fargo

took the ore from him. "No wonder Finnian Mackenzie wouldn't trade his gold in."

Gheller didn't appreciate the slur. "I'm a businessman, not a charity. And I won't stay in business if I don't make a profit on every transaction. If you don't like the arrangement, you can do the same as Mackenzie did and get the hell out."

"Don't mind if I do." Fargo hoped he sounded reasonably angry. Grabbing the saddlebags, he shoved the last piece of ore into them and stalked toward the entrance. Prospectors fell over themselves scrambling out of his path. At the door he glanced back and saw Gheller whispering to Riley.

Slipping outside, Fargo ran to the right and on around the building to the rear. He waited to see if anyone had followed, and when no one showed he jogged toward the stream. Shunning lanterns and campfires he soon came to the crossing. Again he checked behind him and thought he glimpsed a shadow flicker between two tents he has passed. Crouching, he waited over a minute, but no one appeared.

Fargo bounded across and hastened on into Aubrick. Where Lodestone had throbbed with vitality and noise, its twin was comatose. A few wives sat outside their tents with their children, enjoying the evening air, but for the most part Aubrick was as quiet at a tomb.

Light glowed in the church window. Fargo walked to the rear door and rapped twice. No one answered so he knocked again, louder. Footsteps preceded a muffled, "Hold your horses."

The door opened. Amanda was bundled in a robe, not her dress. She was taken aback but composed herself and said sarcastically, "I knew you couldn't stay away for long." Leaning against the jamb, she parted the robe just enough to afford him a glimpse of the delights he had forsaken. "Men are like five-year olds. Offer them some candy and they keep coming back for more."

"I'm here to see your brother," Fargo said.

"Arthur?" Miffed, Amanda pulled the edges of the robe over her breasts. "What do you want with him?"

"That's between your brother and me. Is he here?"

"No. Mrs. Carter's youngest took sick with a fever and chills, and he went to comfort them. He'll be gone a while yet." Amanda tried one more time. "Why don't you step into my parlor and we'll talk about how rash you were to run off like you did."

"I'd sooner be scalped," Fargo responded, and wheeled. "I'll pay Arthur a visit tomorrow. By then he'll have heard the news."

"What news?" Amanda inquired. "That you're leaving the valley, I hope. Good riddance. If we never run into each other again it will be too damned soon."

"Remember, you're a lady. Or pretending to be." Waving cheerily to further antagonize her, Fargo departed. Everything had worked out to his satisfaction. By morning word of his strike would be on everyone's tongue. There wouldn't be a man, women or child in Aubrick or Lodestone who wouldn't know he had supposedly struck the mother lode. Those who had been harassing the Mackenzies would shift their attention to him. He would be shadowed everywhere he went instead of Marjorie and Bethany. And the worst of the lot, the callous killer who had backshot Fin Mackenzie, would try to do the same to him. Or so he hoped.

Fargo hiked northward from the church to give the impression he was returning to his claim. As soon as he was clear of Aubrick, though, he intended to swing around to the south to where he had left Beth and the Ovaro. He passed tent after tent, a few lit within by lanterns but most dark, their absent owners over in Lodestone. Only a few more yards and he would leave the camp behind. That was when the patter of footfalls confirmed his plan to set himself up as a target had worked, but a lot sooner than he anticipated.

Gripping the saddlebags with both hands, Fargo whirled. There were two of them, prospectors in ragged clothes, unkempt beards framing their faces. One was huge and as broad as an ox, and unarmed. The other was a scarecrow wielding a bone-handled knife. They had the presence of mind to come at him from two directions,

95

the ox's brawny arms spread wide to grab him while the scarecrow held the knife low, intending to gut him like a fish.

Fargo swung the saddlebags, throwing his entire body and weight into the motion, and was rewarded with a resounding crack as the ore smashed into the ox's jutting jaw. The man dropped like a dead tree limb. It gave the scarecrow momentary pause, and Fargo capitalized by dropping the saddlebags, swiftly bending, and tugging his Arkansas toothpick from the ankle sheath strapped to his right leg. As he uncurled, the scarecrow pounced. The bone-handled knife streaked at his throat. Fargo countered, and their steel blades rang together. Pivoting, he crouched, the double-edged toothpick glittering dully at his waist.

Again the scarecrow paused. "All we want is those saddlebags!" he hissed. "Le us take them and you won't come to harm."

Fargo's response was to wag the toothpick in a small circle, and grin.

"Suit yourself," the scarecrow snarled. He darted in close, his knife weaving a shimmering tapestry of thrusts and slashes.

Backpedaling, Fargo parried and blocked, thwarting every attempt to stab or disembowel him. It made the scarecrow madder. Throwing caution aside, the man became a whirlwind, swinging wildly, seeking to overpower him in a frenzy of unleashed fury. Bounding to the left, Fargo whipped his foot against the other's legs, knocking them out from under him, and as the man fell, raked the toothpick across an exposed shoulder, drawing blood.

Swearing lividly, the scarecrow surged erect. He glanced at a spreading dark stain on his shirt, and growled deep in his throat. "For that you're going to die, mister. You hear me? You're going to die!"

"Talk is cheap," Fargo baited him, and the ruse worked. Once more the man rushed in close, forsaking all caution, a skinny wolverine gone berserk. Fargo side-stepped, pivoted sharply, and embedded the toothpick in scarecrow's torso just below the sternum. He angled the blade upward so the razor tip pierced the man's heart.

Uttering a strangled grunt, the scarecrow transformed to marble. For long seconds he stood immobile, eyes wide in fear of his imminent end.

Fargo wrenched the toothpick out and prudently stepped back. Blood spouted from the wound, drenching the man's shirt, and his mouth moved soundlessly a few times.

Staggering drunkenly, the scarecrow dropped his weapon and whined like a stricken puppy. He stumbled to his knees, and with a monumental effort gurgled, "I don't want to die!" Not a second later he did, pitching onto his face in the dust.

Fargo leaned down over the body and wiped the Arkansas toothpick clean on the scarecrow's pants. That done, he replaced it in the ankle sheath and straightened. Simultaneously iron arms banded by bulging sinews wrapped around him from behind, pinning his own arms to his sides, and he was bodily lifted off the ground and shaken as a bear might shake a marmot.

"You killed my pard, you son of a bitch!"

The ox had recovered sooner than Fargo figured. He tried to break free, but the prospector was immensely strong. Incredible pressure was applied to his rib cage. He could feel them slowly but inevitably caving in. Another minute and they would shatter like so many twigs.

Fargo had to do something, and quickly. He elicited a howl of pain by suddenly slamming a boot down onto the other's instep, then slammed his head back, into the ox's face. The two combined were enough to slacken the ox's grip, and with a powerful surge of both arms, Fargo succeeded in wresting loose.

Blood trickled from the ox's nose. Favoring his hurt foot, he crouched and circled to the right, his arms outspread. He was a wrestler, a grappler who relied on pure brawn to overpower his adversaries. Two inches taller than Fargo, with shoulders several inches wider, he had the sheer bulk to prevail over most opponents. "I'm fixing to snap your neck for what you did to Lute!" he declared.

Fargo balled his fists and braced himself, waiting.

"Him and me went back a long way together," the ox rumbled. "He was the best partner I ever had."

"At murdering people?" Fargo said. He doubted he was the first. The pair were too slick, too deadly.

The ox grinned wickedly. "Only when we had to. There was that feller in New Orleans a year ago who had a wad of bills he kept flashing around. And that guy and his wife in Kansas City not long after. She was the prettiest thing you ever did see. And my, did she ever put up a tussle when we got her down on the ground. After we were done I held her down and Lute slit her throat."

Fargo rotated as the ox circled so the man was always in front of him. He wasn't fooled by the killer's rambling. It was a ploy to catch him off guard.

"There have been a few other folks, here and there. Whenever we needed money or a woman, we just up and took them. No one gave us a lick of trouble. Until now." The ox glanced at his former companion. "Now I have to find me someone to replace Lute. And good men with a knife don't grow on trees."

"Neither do people with brains," Fargo said.

The ox's features twisted in dire wrath and he launched himself forward, his huge arms sweeping inward to enfold Fargo in their grasp. But Fargo wasn't there. Ducking, he sidestepped and landed two swift punches to the kidneys and a third to the spine. That would have been enough to fell most men, but the ox only arched his back in agony, then whipped around at the waist, his oversized arm fully extended.

Fargo was clipped on the chest and sent tottering. Before he could recover, the ox was on top of him. Arms as thick as pythons enclosed him. His feet left the ground as the man heaved upward to deny him purchase.

"I'm going to crack you like a walnut!"

A vise constricted around Fargo, lancing him with torment. He struggled to extricate himself, but the ox might as well have been chiseled from stone. They were face-to-face, nose to bloody nose. The other's rank, beer-laced breath huffed over him as the ox grunted and applied more strength.

"I love it when the bones start to crack and pop! Reminds me of all those critters I crushed as a kid. Dogs and cats and chickens and the like."

Fargo's arms were throbbing, his chest was on fire. He pushed and thrashed and kicked, all to no avail.

"You're weakening!" the ox crowed. "I can tell! Another minute and you'll be lying at my feet like a busted egg."

The devil of it was, the man was right. Fargo ebbed rapidly. He had difficulty breathing and his vision kept blurring and clearing again. In desperation he smashed his forehead into the ox's leering visage. Not once, not twice, but three times in lightning sequence, and at the third blow there was a loud *crunch* and the ox yelped as if he had been stabbed.

"Damn you!" the man roared, and flung Fargo from him. His nose was shattered, his upper lip a ruin. Spitting blood, he bunched his mallet-shaped fists. "You've done got me good and mad!"

Fargo barely had time to set himself before the ox tore into him again. Only instead of grappling, his brutish attacker rained a battering deluge of knuckles as big as walnuts in a fierce onslaught. Fargo was pummeled on the head, the neck, the shoulders. A few more seconds and he would be beaten into the dirt.

Flinging his forearms up to ward off the clubbing blows, Fargo skipped to the left, putting needed space between them.

The ox took a few wild swings that missed, then coiled to spring. "This is where I finish you off, bastard."

Turning slightly so the man wouldn't notice what he did, Fargo dropped his right hand to the butt of his Colt. "You talk too damn much."

"I'm done talking, mister. Make your peace with your Maker." Snorting like an angry bull, the ox sprang.

Fargo streaked the Colt up and around and the barrel

caught the ox full in the temple, jolting him but also jarring Fargo's hand and almost causing the pistol to slip from his grip. A second swing rocked the ox on his heels. Another opened up his cheek. A fourth split an ear as if it were a rotten apple. Dazed, the ox melted to his knees, but Fargo didn't stop. A red haze enveloped him. Delivering blow after blow, he pistol-whipped his attacker into the ground. Ten, fifteen, twenty times the unyielding metal connected. Fargo swung and swung until an unconscious mass of pulped and bruised flesh lay at his feet.

The red haze faded. Blinking, Fargo stepped back, shocked by his own ferocity. Deep lacerations crisscrossed the ox's huge head. The man's nose was half gone, and an ear hung by a thread of skin. Broken teeth filled a mouth rimmed by shreds of what had once been lips. But Fargo felt no remorse. The man was a killer and had reaped what he more than deserved. Fargo extended the Colt to finish the job.

"What in tarnation is going on over there?"

A woman had emerged from a tent sixty feet away and was peering in his direction. Beside her were a small boy and a girl. Quickly, Fargo retrieved the saddlebags and jogged northward. He traveled fifty yards to mislead potential pursuers, then bore to the east for twice that distance. Finally he swung southward as he had originally planned.

A crowd of mostly women and children had gathered around the sprawled forms in the dirt. As Fargo came abreast of them a lanky figure in a black frock coat arrived on the scene.

"Brothers and sisters, what is this?" Arthur had his Bible with him, and clasped it to his bosom in a show of grief. "More senseless loss of life! When will it end?" He scanned those who had gathered. "Who violated the cardinal edict of our camp? Give me the culprit's name so I can banish him from our midst."

The woman with the small boy and girl cleared her throat. "No one got a good look at him, Parson. I was closest, and all I can tell you is I think he wore a white hat."

"You *think*?" Arthur said.

An elderly man rolled the ox and scarecrow onto their backs. "Say, Parson, the skinny feller there is dead, but this other one is still breathin'. He won't be for long, I reckon. Come sunup he'll be fit for plantin'."

"Round up some of your brethren, Brother Pendergast," Arthur directed. "We'll use a few of the planks left over from building the tabernacle to carry these poor souls there. If your prediction holds true, in the morning we'll hold a double funeral service."

Brother Pendergast hurried off.

Fargo took that as his cue to do likewise. He wasn't in the best of shape. His body ached abominably, and his chest spiked with discomfort whenever he inhaled too deeply. His head was a wellspring of pain, his face so sore and raw that when he rubbed a sleeve across his cheek to wipe off drops of blood, he had to grit his teeth against waves of agony.

Fargo had left the Ovaro in a clearing approximately three hundred yards south of Aubrick. As he stepped from the undergrowth into the open space a lithe shadow detached itself from a nearby oak.

"You're back sooner than I thought," Bethany Mackenzie said. "How did it go?"

"By morning everyone will think I'm the richest person in the territory," Fargo responded.

"Then you'd best be careful. The man who murdered my pa won't be the only one after you. Every sidewinder in the valley will be out to find the mother lode. And they won't lose any sleep if they have to carve you up to do it."

"I've already tangled with two of them," Fargo said as he carefully tied the saddlebags on the stallion.

"Are you all right?"

"I'll get by." Finished, Fargo moved toward the stream, saying over his shoulder, "I'll be back in a minute to take you to the canyon." His face was starting to swell and his lower lip felt puffy. He wound through the boles until he came to the bank and descended to a gravel bar ideal for his purpose. Kneeling, he set his hat to one side and plunged his head into the cool water. It brought prompt but fleeting relief, for as soon as he straightened, the pounding redoubled and his face hurt as badly as ever.

A hand fell on his shoulder. "Let me see," Bethany said, hunkering. She had to lean close in the dark. "My God! You look as if you were stomped by a mustang."

Briefly, Fargo detailed his clash with the would-be thieves.

"We tried to talk you out of setting yourself up as a target, remember?" Bethany gently probed with her fingertips. "Your left eye will be half swollen shut come mornin'. And your lip will hurt like the dickens."

Their faces were a finger's width apart. In contrast to the ox's rank breath, Bethany's had a minty scent reminiscent of pine needles. Her eyes glittered in the starlight, and her lips, puckered in concern, were as inviting as ripe raspberries. Unable to resist, Fargo lightly pressed his mouth to hers in a feathery kiss.

For several heartbeats Bethany was transfixed by astonishment. Then she jerked back and placed a palm over her mouth. "What did you do that for?"

"You're beautiful," Fargo said.

"I don't like a man to take liberties with me." Bethany rose. "If you weren't all black and blue, I'd beat you myself." Still covering her mouth, she bolted into the trees.

"This isn't my night," Fargo said to himself. Once more he dunked his head in the pool and held it underwater for as long as he could. When he rose, the chill breeze on his skin invigorated him. Donning his hat, he retraced his steps to the clearing.

Bethany was by the Ovaro, her arms clasped to her waist, the Spencer in the crook of her right elbow. "I'm ready to head back when you are."

"I'm sorry if I upset you," Fargo said, grasping the reins. "As soon as my face heals, you can slap me a few times if it will make you feel better."

Despite herself, Bethany grinned. "I'll consider that a promise and hold you to it." She nervously shifted her weight from one leg to the other. "About that business at the stream, you scared me, doing what you did without any warnin'."

"You were afraid of a kiss?"

Bethany averted her face. "I'm a country gal. We don't do as much sparkin' as I hear city gals do. You'll laugh, but I can count the number of times I've been kissed on one hand." A forced laugh fluttered from her throat. "Not that I don't like kissin', or anything. From what little I've done, it's right pleasant. I just never had much opportunity."

Fargo had lifted his right foot to the appropriate stirrup. Lowering it again, he walked over behind her and put his hands on her shoulders. "You have an opportunity now."

A shudder ran through her. Slowly, haltingly, Bethany turned, her face etched by hunger and doubt. "Why me? Why us? Why this moment, of all moments?"

"Because we're here. Because we want to."

"Is that enough cause? Shouldn't we be in love? Shouldn't we be married so it's all legal and proper?"

Fargo grinned. "In that case you're better off waiting until that handsome prince comes along to sweep you off your feet." He started toward the stallion, but she gripped his wrist.

"Hold on. Like you said, I might be an old maid by then. And I'd like to enjoy kissin' while I'm still young enough for it to mean something." Bethany's throat bobbed. As timid as a newborn fawn, she inched forward until her bosom was against his chest. "Some folks would brand me a hussy for what I'm about to do. But all I want is to know what it's like. To feel what other women feel. Is that so wrong?"

"Only you can answer that question," Fargo said. He refused to take advantage of her innocence. The choice had to be hers and hers alone. "It doesn't have to be with me. It doesn't have to be now."

"If not you, then who? If not now, then when?" Bethany's arms encircled him.

9

As Bethany Mackenzie's warm hands slid over his shoulders, Skye Fargo realized the full implications of her remarks. She had seldom been kissed. She'd had little to do with men. In other words, she had never made love, never shared her body to its fullest extent. Bethany Mackenzie was a virgin.

Given his druthers, Fargo would pick a fallen dove over a green-as-grass girl any day of the week. There was a lot to be said for experience. Virgins were so anxious and afraid the first time, they failed to enjoy themselves as much as they should. But that wasn't the only reason he favored saloon girls. Virgins tended to get the wrong idea about things. They thought if a man was willing to lie with them, the man must care for them, and once they sacrificed their bodies on the altar of love, it was only right and only natural for the man to ask for their hand in wedlock. They tended to overlook the fact that the male craving for female company often—some would say usually—had nothing at all to do with love or any other lofty notions. It was a basic need, the same as the need to eat and drink. In his case, the same as the need to breathe.

Fargo never misled a woman about his intentions if he could help it. He never did as some men were prone to do and lied through his teeth to get a woman into bed. He never let them think there was more to it than there actually was. So now, as Bethany tilted her head and offered her ripe lips, he did what he would never do were she one of the ladies from the *Aces High*. He paused and said, "I want you to know. I'm not looking to get hitched."

Her reply was barely audible. "Me either."

"In a few days I'll ride on out of the valley and likely never see you again. Keep that in mind."

"I already guessed as much."

"I just don't want any hard feelings afterward. One day you'll meet someone who is ready to settle down, someone who—"

Bethany placed a finger on his lips. "Shut up, you fool, and kiss me before I lose my courage."

"Are you sure?"

Her answer was to fuse her mouth to his in a passionate, hungry kiss, a kiss of need as much as desire. Greedily she sucked on his lips, on his tongue, as if she were seeking to devour him alive.

Fargo caressed the backs of her thighs and Bethany voiced a tiny groan. His hands strayed higher, kneading her soft bottom, as her bosom strained against him and her fingers sculpted the muscular contours of his shoulders and back.

Their kiss lasted a good long while. In due course they broke apart, Bethany flushed and panting as if she had run a mile. Her dilated eyes fixed on him in fascination and she said softly, "You do things to me no man has ever done. You make me all tingly and warm in places I've never been tingly and warm before."

"You haven't felt anything yet," Fargo promised, and pulled her to him. Her hot mouth locked onto his and her soft lips widened to admit his tongue. The contact caused him some discomfort, which he ignored. It would take a lot more than a bruised face to keep him from savoring Bethany's physical treats. While their tongues entwined, he removed her hat and ran his fingers through her silken hair.

Bethany's body radiated heat like a miniature sun. Her hands explored him from neck to belt but she was as yet too shy to venture lower. When Fargo's right hand strayed to her right breast and cupped it, she moaned and went weak at the knees. He had to support her until she steadied herself. "Sorry," she whispered. "I thought I was going to faint."

Bending, Fargo scooped her into his arms and moved to a patch of inky shadow under the overspreading oak. He gently deposited her on her back, then stretched out alongside, placing his hat and gun belt by the trunk. Molding his body to hers, he kissed her smooth forehead, her full cheek, and the satiny skin at the base of her throat.

"Ohhh," Bethany purred. "I like it when you do that."

She liked it even more when Fargo roved his mouth to her ear and sucked on the lobe. Her spine arched, and she dug her fingernails into his back. Again he covered a breast, massaging it. Her nipple became as hard as a tack and her hips began to move of their own accord in an age-old rhythm. When he cupped both breasts at once, she rose up off the ground, her mouth parted, her eyes aglow with bliss.

"Ahh. I'm so hot, so very hot."

That she was. Fargo reached for the top button on her homespun shirt and was puzzled when Bethany grasped his wrist. Looking him deep in the eyes, she licked her voluptuous lips.

"Please. Be gentle with me."

"I wouldn't have it any other way," Fargo assured her. He plucked at the button, but she wasn't done.

"I'm still scared. This is all so new to me. I'm afraid I won't do it right. Or that you won't find me attractive."

"The only way I wouldn't find you attractive is if I were dead," Fargo said. "And being nervous is normal." He succeeded in unfastening two buttons before she gripped his wrist again.

"I want you to know how much this means to me, how grateful I am—"

Fargo touched a finger to her mouth. "Now who should hush up?" To forestall another comment he smothered her lips with his and hurriedly undid the rest of the buttons. In a few more moments he had gained access to her twin globes, each a sweet melon unto itself, ripe and round and tasty. He lathered first one, then the other, flicking her nipples with his tongue.

"Yes! Oh my, yes!" Bethany's fingers wrapped in his hair and she rubbed her thighs against his. The friction generated more heat, more urgency, and she lavished kisses on his head and ears.

Sliding lower, Fargo licked a path across her flat stomach to her navel. He inserted his tongue and rimmed it, and she giggled and squirmed. Unclasping her thin belt, he slowly pushed her pants down so as not to frighten her. Her legs were exquisite, superbly proportioned from thigh to ankle. He added her shoes and socks to the growing pile.

Modesty overcame her. Bethany pressed her legs together and shifted slightly to one side, mumbling a few words into her arm.

"What did you say?" Fargo began to shed his shirt and pants.

Bethany wouldn't look at him. "You can be honest with me. If I'm ugly just say so. If you want to stop I won't blame you."

The only thing that kept Fargo from laughing out loud was that she might misconstrue and think he was laughing at her. "You're as beautiful as a woman can be," he said, easing himself against her. "Any man would be honored to be your lover."

"You're not just saying that?"

Fargo rolled her onto her back so they were face to face. "When you and your mother go East, you'll have more suitors than you'll know what to do with. They'll be falling over themselves to ask you out, and it won't have anything to do with your money. It will be because you're beautiful."

Bethany smiled. "It's sweet of you to say that even if it isn't true. I've always thought of myself as plain as sin."

Fargo never ceased to be amazed by the number of lovely women who thought the same. The exceptions were invariably exceedingly vain, and much less appealing because of it. "Someone once told me that we never see ourselves as others see us. You think you're plain, but you're not. The sight of you is enough to excite any man." To prove it, he took her hand and placed it on his rigid pole.

"Oh my!" The whites of Bethany's eyes showed and she trembled like an aspen leaf. She didn't remove her hand, though, and after a bit she girded the gumption to look down. "It's so big. So hard. So smooth." As she spoke she tentatively rubbed her fingers up and down. "Just like marble."

A constriction formed in Fargo's throat and he nearly exploded. The urge climbed when her hand loosely enfolded his member and she began a pumping motion. To take his mind off the delight she was provoking, he covered her right nipple with his mouth and inhaled it. He also placed his right palm on her belly and caressed in ever widening circles that eventually brought his fingers into contact with her nether mound. When his forefingers brushed her moist slip she cooed like a dove.

"Do that again. Please," she was practically begging him.

Fargo needed no urging. As gently as if she were a rose petal, he pried at her womanhood, and once he gained entry, he ran his finger up and down, giving particular attention to her tiny center of carnal sensation. Bethany heaved upward, her legs spreading to grant him freer rein. At his next stroke she clutched him to her as if she were drowning and he was her sole salvation.

"Ah! Ah! I'm so wet! So very hot!"

That she was, a geyser on the verge of spewing. Fargo inched his forefinger up into her and her inner walls enclosed it in rippling folds. She tossed her head back and forth while voicing small sounds of rapture that rose into the night.

Becoming more forceful, Fargo plunged his finger in and almost out, repeating it over and over. Bethany's hips rose with each lance of his finger, matching his tempo. Their lips glued, their tongues met.

How long Fargo indulged in foreplay he couldn't say. He did so for her sake, to heighten her enjoyment, to bring her to the brink of ultimate release. The first time for a woman was always special, the standard by which all others were measured. To deny her the full pleasure she was entitled to would be unfair.

Presently, Fargo added a second finger. Bethany groaned, and thereafter gasped each time his fingers levered inward. Her legs rose up around him and her ankles locked behind his back. She grew wetter by the moment. Her juices drenched his hand. After a suitable interval, when she was virtually beside herself with need, Fargo positioned himself on his knees and aligned his member with her opening.

Their eyes met, and Fargo paused. In hers he read understanding of what was to come and tacit approval for him to take their coupling to new heights. Gripping her hips, he slowly fed his pulsing manhood into her molten center. She was tight, but there was no obstruction. When he was fully sheathed he lay still a while, letting her adjust to the feeling. Her eyes were closed, and tiny tears had formed at each corner.

"Are you in pain?" Fargo asked.

Bethany shook her head and the tears trickled down her cheeks. She had to try twice to respond. "I'm in heaven," she whispered. "I never knew it would be like this. I want to cry."

Out of consideration for her, Fargo rocked gently at first. Fulfilling her took priority. It was to his benefit, too, since his climax would be that much more intense. The passage of time blurred, as did the woodland around them. They were adrift in their own world, afloat on an ocean of sensual gratification. Nothing else mattered. There was just the two of them, and their rising ecstasy.

Bethany's hips moved faster and faster. Her breasts jiggling, her mouth a rosy circle, she not only matched his ardor, she exceeded it. She was almost to the brink. It wouldn't take much to send her over the other side.

Bending, Fargo rimmed her right nipple with his teeth. That was all that was needed. Crying out, Bethany erupted in a paroxysm of sexual energy. She came, and came, and came again. At each spurt she cried, "Oh! Oh! Oh!" And just when she had expended herself, just when her body was growing still, Fargo reached his own pinnacle. As he rammed up into her, she looked on him in wonder and awe.

"Ahhh!" Bethany clung to his chest, her cheek pressed to his sternum. She quaked with each lance of his hips. Soon she gushed anew, more violently than before, swept up in a tidal wave of uncontrollable delirium.

Fargo's pain was gone, temporarily obliterated by pleasure. Rocking, always rocking, he was immersed in their union. Gradually he coasted to a stop. Sweat caked his body, and his eyelids were heavy. Rolling off onto his side, he embraced her waist and kissed her chin. "Thank you."

Bethany was a while responding. Out of breath, totally spent, she whispered, *"You're* thanking *me*?" She snuggled her forehead up under his chin and closed her eyes. "I've always said there was something strange about you."

Laughing, Fargo shut his own eyes and listened to the wind rustle the trees. They were far enough from Aubrick that the odds of anyone having heard them were slim. He gauged it safe to doze off for a while, but his rest was curtailed by a low nicker from the Ovaro. Raising his head, he groped for his gun belt. The stallion was gazing into the vegetation on the side of the clearing nearest the stream. Its ears were pricked and its posture told him something was out there.

Hastily dressing, Fargo strapped the Colt around his waist and jammed his hat back on. He glided to the Ovaro, yanked the Henry from the saddle scabbard, and tried to detect whatever it was the pinto had heard. But his ears weren't as acute. It didn't help that the leaves were rustling louder than ever.

Since the Sioux were rarely abroad at night, Fargo suspected a four-legged predator, a cougar, maybe, or a bear. A loud *crack* alerted him to a vague shape skulking along the edge of the stream. That it was human was apparent; that it was a white man was established when Fargo saw a hat. A unique hat only one person in all of Aubrick and Lodestone wore. A bowler.

Darting to Bethany, he covered her mouth with one hand and lightly shook her with the other. She was sluggish to awaken, caught as she was in the grip of lingering lethargy. He shook her again, more forcefully, and she sat bolt upright in bewilderment.

"Not a peep!" Fargo whispered in her ear. "We have company. Gather up your clothes and take my horse into the trees. I think I know who it is, and I'll go see what he's doing here while you get dressed."

"It's another *man*?" Bethany said, aghast, looking down at her near-naked body. Embarrassment lent wings to her feet, within moments she sped into the undergrowth, leading the Ovaro by the reins.

Only when Fargo was sure she was safely hidden did he pivot and steal toward the spot where had seen the man in the bowler. The figure hadn't moved. Keeping low, Fargo relied on the available cover to mask his approach.

The man was anxiously staring northward, a short-barreled revolver in his right hand. His shirttail was out and his shirt unbuttoned.

Fargo knew better than to call out. He was liable to be shot. The only thing worse than a greenhorn with a gun was a greenhorn with a *cocked* gun. He slunk close enough to confirm it was who he thought it was, then pressed the Henry's muzzle against the back of Perry Hutchings's neck.

The Chicago detective stiffened and threw up his arms. "How did you sneak up on me like that? I didn't hear a thing. Whoever you are, can't we talk about this? Did the parson send you?"

Fargo sidled around so Hutchings could see him. "It's me. I didn't want to spook you and have you start throwing lead." He lowered his rifle. "What are you doing out here at this time of night?"

Beaming in relief, Hutchings grabbed his wrist. "You! Thank God! I thought I was done for." He rose on his toes to look toward Aubrick. "I'm being followed. Someone is out to kill me."

Crouching, Fargo pulled the detective down beside him. "You've seen them?" he whispered. "Who is it?"

"I don't know. But they've been stalking me for the past quarter of an hour." Hutchings kept his voice low, too.

"Start at the beginning," Fargo instructed.

"I was in my tent, about to turn in, when I heard footsteps. Somebody was sneaking around outside. I went out, but they were too clever for me and had disappeared. So I tied the flap, blew out my lantern, and laid on my cot." Hutchings nervously scanned the forest. "I couldn't sleep. After a while I got up to write a report to my superior in Chicago. And it's well I did. I heard the footsteps again. And the sound of a revolver being cocked."

"But you didn't see who it was?" The only ones Fargo could think of who would want to do the detective harm were Amanda and Arthur Sutton.

"I tried. I opened the flap and jumped outside, but no one was there." Hutchings wiped a sleeve across his perspiring brow. "I knew I hadn't imagined it. So I circled around to try and find whoever was sneaking about. But all I saw were a few women and a couple of old men."

"How did you wind up so far from Aubrick?"

"I was heading back to my tent when I spotted someone off in the darkness, aiming a pistol at me. I ducked before he could fire, then ran, thinking to lose him among the tents and buildings. I thought I had, and I stopped behind the general store to catch my breath." Hutchings swallowed hard. "Next thing I knew, a knife flew out of nowhere and stuck in the wall an inch from my head. So I kept running."

Fargo peered into the night. It took considerable skill to throw a knife accurately, more skill than he imagined Arthur or Amanda possessed. Was someone else after the detective? "Have you made any enemies since you arrived? Besides the Suttons?"

"None that I know of," Hutchings answered. "Unless you count Slan Gheller. He didn't like the questions I asked him and practically threw me out of his saloon." A slight noise to the northwest caused him to crouch lower. "There's something strange going on between those three, but for the life of me I don't have any idea what it is."

"Between Gheller and the Suttons?"

Hutchings nodded. "The first night I was here, I peeked into the church and saw them all huddled together, as friendly as you please. Yet everyone claims they're always at each other's throats." He abruptly flung out an arm. "What's that?"

Fargo swung around. Thirty feet away, on the other side of the stream, something moved. He couldn't say with certainty what it was. It might be a person. It might be an animal. His best bet was to get the detective to the Ovaro, and get out of there.

The matter was taken out of Fargo's hands by the crack of a shot. A slug narrowly missed Hutchings, gouging into a spruce to his left. Instantly Hutchings returned fire, shooting wildly, and then throwing himself flat.

Fargo ducked behind a tree. Levering a cartridge into the Henry's chamber, he scoured the murky vegetation for signs of the bushwhacker, but whoever it was had gone to ground.

"That was too damn close for comfort," Hutchings whispered.

"We can make a fight of it or back off and work our way to Aubrick," Fargo mentioned. "Your choice." Personally, he never liked to sit on his haunches and let an enemy come to him. But to reach the gunman, he had to cross the stream. Any halfway-competent marksman would be able to put two or three slugs into him before he gained the other side.

"I'm not used to this," Hutchings said anxiously. "To the woods, I mean. I'm a city boy. It puts me at a disadvantage."

"Slide back toward me, then," Fargo said. "We'll collect my horse and my friend and light a shuck."

"Your friend?"

From high weeds not eight feet off came another whisper. "That would be me, mister. Bethany Mackenzie. What the devil is going on here, Skye? I came on the run when I heard the shots. Thought maybe you were tanglin' with some Sioux."

"This gent is Perry Hutchings. He's on our side," Fargo explained, "and someone is out to make wolf meat of him."

"Did I understand her correctly?" Hutchings asked. "Did she say there are *Indians* in this vicinity?"

Bethany answered herself. "Hell, mister. Where are you from? The moon? This whole territory is crawlin' with hostiles. One of these days they'll take it into their heads to drive all the whites out and the prairie will run red with blood."

"Give me Chicago any day," Hutchings muttered. "The worst we have are footpads and roughnecks. No Indians, no rattlesnakes, no bears, no cougars, no swarms of mosquitoes trying to eat you alive—"

"Sounds like a nice place," Bethany said. "I'd like to hear more about it."

Fargo seemed to be the only one keeping an eye out for the gunman. "Some other time," he said more harshly than he intended. "Follow me, Hutchings. And whatever you do, stay down."

"You can count on that," the greenhorn said. The words were hardly out of his mouth when he rose halfway up off the ground. The moment he did, the bushwhacker across the stream snapped off two shots. At the first, Hutchings's bowler hat bounced into the air as if kicked. At the second, the detective clutched at his arm and fell onto his chest. "I've been hit!"

Fargo had seen a spurt of flame and smoke. As rapidly as he could, he sent four shots into the spot where the man must be. No yips of pain greeted his volley, nor did he hear the thud of a body striking the earth. "Can you crawl?" he whispered.

"I think so. My arm is going numb, but I can manage." Hutchings started to snake toward a thicket, then stopped and scoured the grass. Spying his bowler, he twisted to retrieve it.

"Don't!" Fargo warned.

More blasts boomed, but this time some of the shots came from the same side of the stream they were on, from a cluster of cottonwoods fifty feet to the north. Perry Hutchings cried out and flipped backward. He had been hit again.

"Damn." Fargo burst into the open, pumping the Henry's lever fast and furious. To pin the ambushers down he fired twice at the gunman on the other side of the stream and twice at the gunman to the north. Tucking at the knees, he hoisted Hutchings up off the grass, but they hadn't covered three yards when the assassin on their side let loose with three more shots, one after the other.

Buzzing lead blistered the air. Fargo felt a slight tug on his shoulder, but the slug had merely creased his buckskins. Using the Henry one-handed, he returned fire even though he couldn't hold the rifle all that steady. Fortunately, Bethany Mackenzie rushed to their aid. Barreling out of the weeds, she added the Spencer to the fray, squeezing off rounds as rapidly as any man.

The gunman to the north of the stream got off one last shot just a Fargo hauled Hutchings into a belt of pines. The greenhorn had gone limp. Crouching, Fargo felt for a pulse. It was there, strong but slow. He searched for bullet holes and found one high on the detective's shoulder and a nasty furrow along Hutchings's right temple.

Bethany backed up beside him, the Spencer tucked to her side. "How's the pilgrim? Alive or dead?"

"He'll live, but he needs doctoring." Fargo handed the Henry to her, slipped both arms under Hutchings, and carried him to the clearing. "I'll lend you my pinto. Take our friend here to the canyon and look after him until I get there."

"Ma won't like me totin' a stranger home."

"Tell her it was either that or have him murdered in his tent by the same people who murdered Fin." Fargo was in a hurry. He placed Hutchings belly-down over the saddlebags, then boosted Bethany into the stirrups and gave her the reins. "With any luck I'll be there by morning." Fishing a box of ammo from his saddlebags, he stepped back.

Bethany had no need to ask what he was going to do. Leaning down, she caressed his cheek. "Don't let anything happen to that handsome head of yours, hear? I've taken a shine to it."

"I'll try my best," Fargo said, and sprinted off.

The hunters were about to become the hunted.

10

Skye Fargo had replaced the spent cartridges in the Henry and was shoving the box of ammunition into a pocket when the telltale crackle of dry pine needles pinpointed the position of one of the bushwhackers. A spectral shape flitted from tree to tree like some great ebony moth, angling in his general direction. Fargo fixed a bead as best he could, but at the exact instant he curled his forefinger around the trigger the figure vanished behind a pine. Expecting it to reappear on the other side, he shifted and sucked in a breath. But seconds dragged by and the gunman never materialized.

Puzzled, Fargo scoured the area. Through a break in the growth he spied the stream, and as his gaze alighted on it, the other bushwhacker stepped from concealment and started across. Fargo already had the rifle leveled, so all he had to do was point it and squeeze the trigger. But once more, as he was about to shoot, the person melted into thin air.

Fargo was beginning to think they truly must be Sioux. Sioux warriors were masters at blending into the terrain. He squatted, the better to spot them, and instead spotted three other figures moving southward along the far bank. Apparently he wasn't the only one who saw them. To the south a revolver spat lead but not at him. One of the three newcomers staggered and called out, "They've plugged me!" At that, the third man leaped in front of the others and cut loose with unbelievable speed and precision, five shots fired so swiftly they sounded as a single continuous blast.

Only one person in the entire valley possessed enough skill to employ a six-shooter so artfully, only one person other than Fargo. It had to be Cass Benedict, which meant the other two were Riley and young Kenny.

Benedict's shots were directed at the spot the ambusher had fired from and they must have come close because the next moment the lurker in the trees raced eastward heedless of the noise he made.

Fargo gave chase. He didn't know what Gheller's gunnies were doing there, or why one of the killers who tried to slay Perry Hutchings had fired at them. But he would find out if he could catch the two-legged mountain goat bounding ahead of him. He ran flat out, hurtling a series of obstacles; a log here, a boulder there, a stump further on. They were passing through a particularly dense tract of woodland, and all he had were fleeting glimpses of his quarry. But the glimpses were enough to convince him the one he was after wasn't a man at all. The way the person moved, the sway of their body and their light, flowing gait, suggested it was a woman. A woman dressed in black from hair to toe, including a black hat and veil. He saw them clearly when she became aware she was being pursued and glanced over a shoulder as she was crossing an open space.

"Amanda," Fargo deduced aloud.

Without warning the woman in black stopped and rotated, a revolver glinting dully in her hand. Fireflies flared, accompanied by false thunder.

A log offered Fargo protection from the leaden hailstorm. He flung himself behind it, and when the thunder ended with a loud *click,* he was up and running again, resolved to catch her no matter what. But damn, she was fast. He never would have thought Amanda had it in her. The speed with which she navigated the benighted maze, the ease with which she vaulted obstructions were worthy of an Apache maiden. He had taken her for a city girl, as inept in the woods as Perry Hutchings.

A thought struck Fargo, and he reached deep inside himself, into his reservoir of stamina, to narrow the gap even more. They were racing in the same direction Bethany and Hutchings had gone. While normally the stallion could ride rings around a human, Bethany had been holding to a walk so as not to unduly jostle her wounded charge. It wasn't inconceivable Amanda might overtake them before too long. Perhaps that had been her intention all along, and her exchange of lead with Gheller's gun sharks had been to prevent them from interfering.

If Fargo was right about it being Amanda, the other bushwhacker had to be her brother. Arthur was the one who shot Hutchings in the arm, and he must still be in the general area. Yet another surprise. Fargo had pegged the so-called parson as a coward whose only weapons were lies and trickery, but here Arthur was, roaming the woodland at night when most were too scared to set foot in it, and proving he could shoot as skillfully as he was able to quote passages from Scripture.

Absorbed in thought, Fargo had let his gaze stray from Amanda. Now, glancing up, he was startled to discover she had evaporated into thin air. Acting on the assumption she had flattened and was lying in ambush, he slowed and advanced as cautiously as a cat in a room full of dogs. He reached out with his senses, testing for sounds, scents, for anything out of the ordinary, and his ears rewarded him with the soft *crunch* of a twig. The only thing was, it came from off to his left, not from straight ahead.

Arthur! Fargo realized, and pivoted. The brother's lanky black-garbed silhouette was almost invisible against the backdrop of dark forest, but he spotted it a split second before a pistol hammered and a slug hummed past his ear. He answered in kind, with the Henry, and the silhouette was swallowed by undergrowth. But whether because his shots brought Arthur low or Arthur had sought cover was unknown.

In a twinkling another gun joined the litany of death. Amanda, to help her sibling, triggered three shots, and it was a testimony to her marksmanship that all three clipped whangs from Fargo's shirt. Trying to locate her, he dropped into a crouch, but she was too smart to fire when he was expecting her to.

Now he didn't know where either one of them was.

By rights Fargo should stay put until he was certain it was safe. But he was worried about Bethany, concerned she might take it into her pretty head to ride back and lend him a hand. If she did, she would ride straight into the Suttons, who wouldn't hesitate to blast her from the saddle and finish off Hutchings. So, discarding caution, he continued on, doubled at the waist to minimize the target he presented. Twenty yards he traveled, but no shots rang out. Forty yards, and he concluded he was wasting his time.

Amanda and Arthur had given him the slip.

It bothered Fargo to think a pair of Easterners had gotten the better of him. Two greenhorns who had spent most of their lives in cities and towns had outwitted him in his own element, the wilderness he called home. Were they Comanches or Cheyenne he wouldn't be nearly so upset. Either he was slipping, or there was a lot more to the Suttons than Perry Hutchings had revealed. Or was aware of.

Wheeling, Fargo hastened toward the stream. The gunshots had silenced all the coyotes and owls and other wildlife, and the valley lay serene under a celestial canopy. He wasn't surprised that no one from Aubrick or Lodestone had investigated the gunfire. The men in the saloon probably hadn't heard it, and the women and children in the tents weren't about to venture beyond the camp's safe haven.

A string of curses brought Fargo to a stop. He was near the spot where Amanda had swapped lead with Gheller's gunnies. Proceeding noiselessly, he crept to a bush at the edge of the stream. On a flat bank on the other side lay the gunman who had been shot. A second man had knelt and was examining his shoulder.

"Damn you, Riley! Quit poking so hard!" It was the young one, Kenny. "It hurts worse now than it did when you began poking and prodding."

"It has to be done, lad," Riley said. "If the slug is still in there I'll have to dig it out."

"Like hell you will. Help me back to Lodestone and

rustle up that old geezer who claims he was a sawbones years ago. Wilson, his name is. He's the closest thing to a doc we've got."

"We'll go as soon as Cass returns."

Fargo raked the forest beyond them for sign of the small gunman. He needn't have looked quite so far, for suddenly he sensed someone was behind him, and he knew who it was without turning. "First the parson's sister, now you. Next time I visit Denver, I'm having my eyes and ears checked."

"What makes you think you'll live that long?" Cass Benedict asked. He sidled around on the right, his ivory-handled Colt an extension of his palm.

"You're not like those two," Fargo said, nodding at the pair across the stream. "According to the stories I've heard you only kill when you have to, and you always give the other guy a chance to go for his gun first." Fargo slowly rose, the Henry pointed down. "I'm surprised you'd work for someone like Gheller."

Benedict's features were mired in shadow. For a bit he didn't say anything, then he responded, "Blame a run of bad luck at cards. I needed money to stake myself, and Gheller offered me a lot to be his top gunhand for a while."

Water splashed loudly as Riley came wading across, unlimbering his Remington. "I'll be damned, Cass! You've caught the one gent our boss most wants to pound into the dirt. Well, excepting the parson, of course." He clambered onto the bank. "Say the word and I'll shoot him in the leg so he's less likely to give us trouble on the way back."

"You're taking me to Lodestone?" Fargo said.

"Whether you like it or not," Riley gleefully declared. "You have a lot to answer for, mister. Fist Mort, now Kenny."

"Amanda shot your friend. Not me."

"The parson's sister? You're saying she was the one who threw down on us? How stupid do you think I am?"

"Do you really want to know?"

Riley raised his long-barreled Remington. "Let me put a slug into this son of a bitch, Cass. Just one, is all I ask."

"No. Relieve him of his hardware," Benedict said. "Then help Kenny up."

Scowling, Riley circled behind Fargo and jammed the Remington against Fargo's backbone. "One twitch, mister," he hissed. "One twitch and you'll be using crutches the rest of your life." Slowly reaching around, he snatched the Colt and wedged it under his own gun belt. A moment later he took the Henry. "Let's see how mouthy you are with your claws clipped." Laughing sadistically, he gouged the Remington deeper.

In the blink of an eye, Fargo sidestepped and spun, smashing the back of his fist into the pudgy gunman's chin.

Caught flat-footed, Riley was propelled half a dozen feet and landed on his backside. More humiliated than hurt, he leaped right back up, snarling like a beast. Jabbing the Remington at Fargo, he railed, "No one does that to me. You hear? I'm going to shoot that hand plumb off."

"No," Cass Benedict said.

"No?" Riley was almost beside himself. "You saw what he did! You wouldn't let anyone hit you and get away with it. Why should I? If I want to shoot him to pieces, I damn well will!"

"No, you won't."

For tense seconds the two gunmen stared at each other, locked in a silent conflict of wills. It was Riley who gave in, who shrugged and thinly smiled and said with a tinge of resentment, "The boss says we're to do what you tell us, so I reckon I don't have any choice. But you're in the wrong in this, Cass, and we both know it."

"Help Kenny up," Benedict said.

The young gunny had been listening and called out, "About time! I'm over here bleeding to death and the two of you are squabbling like a couple of women. Hurry it up. I hurt something awful."

Riley waded back across, mumbling fiercely to himself. Fargo crossed the stream and fell into step between

Riley and Kenny. The latter was too weak to walk unassisted. They moved at a snail's pace, Kenny whimpering every few yards.

"Listen to you," Riley said in disgust. "If you were any more puny you'd be wearing a diaper."

"Easy for you to say," Kenny marshaled through clamped teeth. "You're not the one with a slug in you."

"Hell, lad. I've been shot before, and I never carried on as you are." Burdened by the Henry, Riley awkwardly supported the younger man with both arms. "I'll get a stick for you to bite down on if you reckon that will help you act your age."

"Go to hell."

"Don't be mad at me. It wasn't my idea to come traipsing out here in the dead of night. Had it been up to me, we'd never have left the comfort of the Aces High and you would never have been shot."

Fargo seized the opening to ask, "Whose idea was it? Gheller's?"

"None of your damn business," Riley said. "From here on out keep your mouth shut or I'll shut it for you."

Again Cass Benedict intervened. "He can talk if he wants."

Riley glanced back. "What the hell has gotten into you, hoss? Why are you sticking up for him? You know as well as I do what the boss will do. He's a walking dead man, hardly worth your bother."

"Why does Gheller plan to kill me?" Fargo asked. As if he couldn't guess.

"You're not as smart you think you are. There are things going on you know nothing about."

Fargo wondered what Riley was referring to.

"As for you," Riley said, helping Kenny over an exposed root, "the boss wants to know where that mother lode is and he'll do whatever it takes to pry the secret out of you." He emphasized, "Whatever it takes."

"Slan Gheller has no scruples whatsoever about killing," Cass Benedict said. "The only reason he never had Marjorie or Bethany Mackenzie staked out and tortured is his fondness for the girl."

"The boss is a master at it," Riley bragged. "I've been with him longer than anyone else, so I should know. Once I saw him skin a man alive. Another time, he cut out a fella's eyes, and when that didn't work, he cut off the nose and ears. It still didn't loosen the guy's tongue so the boss had me undo the lunkhead's britches and he went to work between the guy's legs." Riley laughed. "You should have heard the screams! Reminded me of a stuck pig. In the end he told us what the boss wanted to know, so he went through all that for nothing. It's amazing how dumb some people are."

A whole new aspect to Slan Gheller had been revealed, an aspect Fargo never suspected existed. "What did you mean by things going on that I know nothing about?"

"Wouldn't you like to know," Riley mocked him. "We'll let the boss fill you in. I wouldn't want to spoil his fun."

Fargo looked at Cass Benedict. "And you approve of what your employer does? Those newspaper accounts painted you as a man of honor, but I guess they were wrong."

"I do what I'm paid to do," Benedict said. "But there are lines I won't cross. I made that clear to Gheller before he hired me."

"He sure did." This from Riley. "I thought for sure the boss would tell him to take a hike when you rattled off all that stuff."

"What stuff?" Fargo quizzed.

"The great Cass Benedict," Riley said in contempt. "He never hurts women. He never hurts kids. He doesn't backshoot. When he kills someone he has to be facing them." Riley snorted. "You'd think *he* was the parson, the way he puts on airs."

The small gunman's voice was gravel on tin. "The last man who talked about me like that is pushing up daises in a cemetery."

Riley tried to backpedal. "To each their own, I always say. If you want to go through life living by some silly code that's your business. Me, I don't pretend to be more than I am. I kill folks. It doesn't matter who. It doesn't matter where. Gheller says to do it and I do it. Simple and sweet."

"Even women and children?" Fargo asked.

"What difference does that make? Sure, I've done a few in my time. I'm not exactly partial to it, though, like Mort was. Whenever the boss needed a gal or a brat disposed of, Mort begged for the job. Why, down to Santa Fe one time, he strangled the prettiest girl you ever did see. She couldn't have been more than seventeen."

Fargo was now doubly glad he had gunned Mort down. The sidewinder would only have gone on murdering more innocents.

"No one ever mentioned any of this to me," Cass Benedict commented.

"Why should we?" Riley retorted. "You're the new man in the outfit. Maybe the boss thinks highly of you, but the rest of us don't much cotton to your highfalutin airs. To be honest, some of us downright hate your guts. Mort hated you most of all. Were it up to him, your carcass would be nothing but bleached bones by now."

Fargo was constantly scanning the undergrowth on the left for a convenient spot to make a break. Once they got him into Lodestone it would be too late. But the woods were eight or nine feet from the stream. To reach over without being shot was impossible.

Kenny raised his head and tried to twist around, but he couldn't muster the energy. "Riley doesn't speak for all of us, Cass," he commented. "You've always treated us decent, and I, for one, have always looked up to you."

"Kiss his ass, why don't you?" Riley said bitterly. "You only like him because he's faster on the draw than anyone you've ever seen. If he was as slow as molasses you wouldn't think any better of him than I do."

Fargo glanced at Cass Benedict. "Having second thoughts yet?"

"Let's just say I wouldn't have hooked up with Gheller if I'd known then what I know now. But it doesn't change things where you're concerned. When he hired me, I gave my word to abide by his decisions. He wants you brought to him and that's exactly what I aim to do."

"It doesn't matter if the man you've given your word to isn't worthy to lick your boots?" Fargo asked.

"It's not who you give it to, it's *giving* it that's important," Benedict responded. "When I say I'll do something I'm obliged to do it whether I want to or not." Under his breath, so the other two gunmen couldn't hear, he said, "Damn me for a fool. I'd stopped hiring out my gun years ago. I should have found some other way to raise a stake."

"Empty pockets have a way of leading men astray," Fargo observed. As well he should know. There had been times when he had been down on his luck and taken jobs he would never have thought twice about taking if he were flush.

The lights of Lodestone blazed ahead. To the northeast sparkled its twin, Aubrick. Another couple of minutes and they would be there.

"I'm starting to get dizzy," Kenny said weakly. "Go faster, Riley, or I'll be dead before we get there."

"Hang on, lad. It won't be long."

The pudgy gunman picked up the pace and Fargo had to do the same. The heavy vegetation ended, and so did any hope Fargo had of making a bid to elude the gunmen. Riley and Kenny started across an open field. His only recourse now was to jump Cass Benedict. But with the ivory-handled Colt six inches from his back, any attempt to overpower the small gunman was bound to have only one outcome.

"The pain is growing worse, too," Kenny mewed. "It feels as if the bullet is grinding against my collar bone."

"As soon as we reach the shack I'll go after Doc Wilson," Riley said. "I'll drag him there if I have to, but he'll get there."

Raucous laughter and tinny music wafted from the saloon. Relatively few of the tents were lit inside. Of those, one was larger than all the rest and bore a sign that read, BIG NOSE KATE. FIVE MINUTES, FIVE DOLLARS. In front of it ten or eleven prospectors were lined up waiting their turn.

Fargo tried to see inside, but the flap was closed.

"All of Gheller's women have to sell themselves," Cass Benedict remarked. "They're allowed to keep twenty-five percent of what they earn. The rest goes to him."

North of the Aces High stood a shack. Riley worked a rusty latch, kicked the door open, and crossed a musty room to a well-worn cot in a far corner. He slowly eased Kenny down, leaned the Henry against the wall, and bustled to a pine table that had seen better days. Striking a match, he lit a lantern caked with dust.

Fate had granted Fargo one last chance. He stopped in the doorway, waiting for Cass Benedict to come up behind him. If he timed it right, a quick spring was all it would take. He tensed his legs and shifted slightly, but Benedict inadvertently thwarted him by halting a few yards back.

Riley indicated a chair in the center of the room. "What are you waiting for, mister? A formal invite? Have a seat. We'll make you nice and comfortable." He took a coil of rope from a peg over the cot.

Fargo stared at the unwavering ivory-handled Colt in Benedict's hand, and complied.

"Be sure to tell me if this hurts and I'll make it hurt worse," Riley gloated. Hunkering, he tied Fargo's wrists to the chair arms and his ankles to the front legs, none too gently. When he was done he yanked hard on each loop. "How does it feel being trussed up like a lamb for the slaughter?"

"Go get Gheller," Benedict instructed.

"And Wilson!" Kenny chimed in from the cot. "Don't forget old Doc Wilson. Have him bring that bag of his."

Riley ran out. Cass Benedict moved to the only other chair and straddled it so he was facing Fargo. Only then did he twirl his revolver into its silver-studded holster. "What happens next is out of my hands."

"Is that what you'll tell yourself so you can sleep at nights?" Fargo said, unable to conceal his anger.

Benedict pulled his hat brim lower over his eyes. "We

all do things we're not proud of. I reckon that includes you."

"When I was younger I did a lot I'm not proud of," Fargo admitted. "But now I know better. What's your excuse?"

"Damn it," Benedict snapped. "Try putting yourself in my boots. If the situation were reversed you'd do exactly as I am."

"Would I?" Fargo said. "Or would I have the grit to stand on my own two feet and not be bound by my word to a man who doesn't deserve my loyalty?"

Cass Benedict said nothing.

Recognizing it was hopeless, Fargo strained his ears for footfalls. He didn't have long to wait. The door opened again and in clomped Riley. With him were two more gunmen, unsavory characters Fargo had seen in the saloon earlier, more of Slan Gheller's hired gunslicks. Last to saunter in was Gheller himself, smiling in that grandfatherly manner of his, all oil and charm as he came over and hooked his thumbs in his vest.

"My, my. How fickle fortune can be. One minute we're on top of the world, the next we're staring death in the face." Gheller leaned down. "Make no mistake about it. You *will* die if you don't tell me what I want to know."

"You'll kill me no matter what I do," Fargo said.

Gheller's chortled. "True. But it will go a lot easier for you if you cooperate. Instead of whittling on you until you beg me to end your suffering, I'll have one of my men put a bullet through your skull. How would that be?"

Fargo had a sharp retort on the tip of his tongue, but Kenny spoke first.

"What about me, boss? Didn't Riley tell you I've been shot? Where's Wilson? I need to have a slug dug out."

"I sent Cavendish for Wilson," Gheller said. "The old bag is sleeping off a bender in his tent. It'll take a while to sober him up to where he can work on you without botching it."

"Have them hurry. Please. I'm feeling worse by the minute."

Gheller wasn't listening. He had reached into an inside jacket pocket and pulled out a folding knife. Opening it, he held the blade so it caught the lantern light. "Where should I start, Trailsman? With an eye? With your nose?" He glanced at the left chair arm. "I know." Suddenly, gripping Fargo's thumb, Gheller held it so Fargo couldn't pull loose. "How about if we start with this?" He touched the razor edge of the knife to the skin just above the knuckle.

11

Skye Fargo had stared death in the face many times. Cutthroats, hostile Indians, and every sort of vicious beast known to man had at one time or anther tried to end his life. He accepted the fact it was part and parcel of the life he had chosen, that danger and the frontier went hand-in-hand and every day might be his last. But he'd always hoped that when his end came it would be quick. Maybe a bullet or an arrow to a vital organ, or maybe a grizzly would jump him and crush his skull like an overripe melon. He never figured on being tortured to death, at least not by whites. Apaches and a few other tribes indulged in the practice, but he never expected to be taken alive.

Fargo steeled himself as Slan Gheller's knife pressed lightly against his thumb, breaking the skin. He refused to cry out, refused to give Gheller and Riley and the other two grinning gunnies the satisfaction of seeing him whimper or grovel. He would die as he had lived, with his head held high, with a degree of dignity if with nothing else.

"What's it to be?" Gheller asked. "Do I cut this off? Or will you tell me where you found the mother lode?"

"I'll tell you," Fargo said.

"You will? Just like that?" Gheller's brows pinched together. "I'm disappointed. I thought it would take a lot more to loosen your tongue. Either you're smarter than I gave you credit for or you're more yellow than most folks say." He removed the blade from Fargo's thumb. "Out with it, then! You know how much I want the damn gold. How do I go about finding the mother lode?"

"You shove your hand up your ass."

Cass Benedict laughed, but the other gunmen didn't find it anywhere near as amusing. Certainly Slan Gheller didn't. Transfixed by rage, he stood stock still, his fleshy features growing darker and darker until he resembled a steam boiler about to burst. Then he snarled and lowered the knife again, holding it just above Fargo's thumb. "For that you'll pay. A minute from now you'll have nothing but stumps where your fingers used to be." He looked down. "I'm going to cut nice and slow so you feel every slice."

Several loud knocks abruptly shook the door. Gheller swore in annoyance and called out, "Is that you, Cavendish? How the hell did you sober the doc up so fast?"

"It's not Cavendish," said the last person in the world Fargo ever imagined would set foot in Lodestone.

"Arthur?" Astonishment straightened Gheller. For the moment he forgot about hacking off Fargo's fingers. Pivoting, he motioned at Riley and the other pair, who fanned out, their hands above their gun butts.

Cass Benedict stood and moved over by the wall, lounging against it with his arms folded. His posture and calm were misleading. As quick as he was, he could draw and fire before any of the rest cleared leather.

"We need to talk," Arthur declared. "Open up."

Fargo noticed something as Gheller closed the folding knife and stepped to the door. Gheller was scared. So were Riley and the other two hardcases. They were trying hard not to show it, but they were afraid. It made no sense. Arthur and his sister had murdered a few people, but Gheller and the gunmen were killers themselves.

Slan Gheller plastered a smile on his face and lifted the latch. "This is a surprise. You have some nerve coming here after the stunt you tried to pull."

Arthur Sutton slowly entered. Under his frock coat he wore a black shirt instead of the usual white one, and on his head rested a black broad-brimmed hat. Strapped around his skinny waist was a black gun belt. "What stunt would that be?" he responded. His voice, his whole bearing, had changed. An aura of menace clung to him, and he looked on Riley and the other two with disdain.

After him came his sister. Amanda, too, had undergone a remarkable transformation. In place of her lacy dress she wore an outfit much like Arthur's. She had added a veil, the ends were attached to the brim of her hat. Only her eyes were visible. Cold, emotionless eyes that alighted on Fargo and gleamed with devilish hatred. She, too, wore a gun belt tied low.

"What do you take me for?" Gheller demanded. "You know very well what stunt." He pointed at Fargo. "The two of you tried to trick him into killing me. You told him I was out to get you."

"All part of our act," Arthur said. "Of deceiving everyone into thinking you and I are enemies so they'd never suspect the truth."

"You do remember our pact, don't you?" Amanda said. "We agreed to work together to fleece the prospectors of every ounce of gold they found. Us in our way in Aubrick, you in yours over here."

Gheller resented her tone. "Don't patronize me. Our deal was that you would keep a list of their strikes and let me know who has the most gold so I can have my gals lure them into losing it at my tables. In return I agreed to cut you in for half. Between that and the tithes you've imposed on your so-called flock, you're making almost as much money as I do."

"A profitable arrangement for all of us," Arthur said.

"But a pittance compared to the mother lode," Amanda remarked. "As for him," she nodded at Fargo, "he's smarter than most. He was becoming suspicious. We had to do something to throw him off the scent so we fed him a cock-and-bull story about you having it in for us."

"Putting my life at stake," Gheller said testily.

"We knew you wouldn't be stupid enough to give him cause to gun you down," Arthur said.

"And we intended to warn you," Amanda said, "but

he paid you a visit before my brother could sneak on over here."

"How thoughtful." Gheller still wasn't satisfied. "But I find it hard to believe you have my best interests at heart when half an hour ago you shot Kenny." He nodded toward the cot. "Explain that if you can."

Amanda shrugged. "How were we to know who it was? We were after Hutchings and saw three men coming toward us. We took them for interlopers and did what we had to."

"Which makes us wonder," Arthur said. "What were your hired guns doing there? Did you sic them on us?"

"Of course not," Gheller said, and laughed long and loud. A little too long, and a little too loud.

Fargo knew Gheller was lying, and he had a strong hunch the siblings did, too. Yet neither made an issue of it. They weren't the least bit angry or offended. Which struck him as strange. Their righteous facade to the contrary, they weren't the sort to forgive and forget. He was going to say as much when a slight creak drew his gaze to the cot.

Kenny had risen and was standing with one hand braced against the wall, his other dangling near his revolver. His face was chalky and beaded with sweat, and he had to moisten his mouth to speak. "Did I just hear right? It was one of you who shot me?"

Amanda shifted toward him. "That would be me," she said. "In the dark my aim was off a bit. Sorry."

"You're *sorry*!?" Kenny exclaimed, furious. He broke into a violent fit of coughing. Crimson drops flecked his lips and dribbled onto his chin, and he almost toppled back onto the cot.

Riley turned and motioned. "Sit down, lad, or you'll do yourself in before the sawbones gets here."

Kenny steadied himself, wiped a sleeve across his chin, and shook his head. "Stay out of this, pard. This is between the bitch and me."

"I'll let that pass," Amanda said cooly. "You don't realize what you're saying. You're in a lot of pain. You're confused—"

133

"Like hell!" Kenny glowered. "You put a slug into me, bitch, and I aim to repay the favor. Whenever you're ready reach for your hardware!"

Now it was Gheller who tried to intercede. "Forget about it, Ken. You don't stand a prayer against her. I told you who these two are, remember?"

Kenny was too hotheaded to heed. "So what if they robbed a few stages and whatnot in Missouri? And so what if they bucked a few folks out with lead? She's just another woman to me. I don't care how many holes I've been plugged with, the day I can't beat a woman to the draw is the day I deserve to be planted."

The mention of Missouri jarred Fargo's recollection of accounts he had heard about a pair of black-garbed outlaws who were the terror of the state for six or seven months about a year ago. A ruthless twosome who shot anyone who so much as looked at them crosswise. Men, women, even a few children had been brutally slain. Eventually the governor assembled a permanent posse to track them down, but no sooner was word of the posse leaked to the newspapers than the robberies ceased. Everyone speculated the pair had moved on to different pastures, and they had been right.

Arthur glanced at his sister. "Did you hear the simpleton? I don't mind handling it, sis. I can use the practice."

"I'm the one he insulted," Amanda said. "I'm the one who should bed him down."

Kenny was struggling to concentrate, struggling to stay on his feet. He was too weak to do it for long, though, and maybe that was why he suddenly cried, "To hell with both of you!" and slapped at his pistol.

One instant Amanda's hand was beside her holster. The next, her revolver spat smoke and lead.

Bored through the sternum, Kenny was punched back against the wall. He gamely drew his pistol, but what little strength he had left had deserted him, and it clattered to the floor as he oozed onto the cot, leaving a red smear in his wake. Whining pathetically, he twitched a few times, then expired.

Amanda spun her revolver into her holster and faced

Slan Gheller. "Now where were we? Oh yes. You were complaining about the little misunderstanding we had with your boys."

Gheller stared at the lifeless husk of his underling. "Why are the two of you here? It sure as hell isn't to pay me a social visit."

"We know where the mother lode is," Arthur said, "and we thought you might want to be with us when we take it away from its rightful owner."

"Just as we agreed months ago," Amanda said.

"How can you know where it is? Fargo would rather lose all his fingers than tell me."

"Him?" Amanda laughed and sashayed to the chair. "He's been playing you for a jackass, Slan. Oh, he knows where it is, but it's his secret to share."

"You've lost me, lady."

Amanda teasingly traced the outline of Fargo's chin with the tip of a finger. "I told you our friend here is smarter than most. The gold he was flashing around wasn't his. It was given to him by the rightful owners of the mother lode. Probably so everyone would go after him instead of them."

"Who are you talking about? Who really found it?"

Arthur grunted. "Honestly, Slan. I wonder about you sometimes. Who else but the Mackenzies? Just as we've always suspected." He grinned at Fargo. "I was upstream today visiting some of the prospectors. To offer spiritual support, of course, and see for myself how much gold they've panned."

"We wouldn't want them to cheat us out of our rightful tithe," Amanda said, and chuckled.

"I went farther than I usually do," Arthur went on. "It got late, and I was tired, so I sat in the shade of a cliff to rest. Lo and behold, who should come walking out of a bunch of big slabs of rock not fifty yards away but our friend, here, and Bethany Mackenzie. I dropped flat and they didn't see me."

"The mother lode was in among those rocks?" Gheller said, suddenly excited.

"No, Slan. Bear with me a moment," Arthur chided.

"You see, I got to wondering what they had been doing, so as soon as they were out of sight, I had a look. And there it was. The answer to the mystery. The secret the Mackenzies have so zealously guarded. The entrance to a hidden canyon."

"It was there? You actually saw the mother lode with your own eyes?"

"Let's not get ahead of ourselves, shall we?" Arthur said. "I was in my parson's outfit. I wasn't armed. Knowing how quick the Widow Mackenzie is on the trigger, I had to be careful. I spotted what looked like a cave, and the widow, herself, drinking coffee by a fire." He paused. "That's where the mother lode has to be, Slan. In that cave. Ours for the taking."

"The Mackenzies won't give it up without a fight," Amanda said, "and that's where you and your men come in. Between all of us we can dispose of them easy as pie."

"What do you say, Slan?" Arthur inquired. "Are you in?"

"Need you ask?" Gheller rubbed his palms together, his face agleam with greed. "When do you want to leave? I can have all my boys mounted and ready to go in fifteen minutes."

"That's more than enough time," Arthur said. "Sis and I have a few things to attend to. We'll meet you at the first bend of the stream north of Aubrick."

Gheller headed for the door, barking orders like a military commander. "Cass, round up the rest of the men. Riley, have all the horses saddled and out in front of the saloon, pronto. Dixon, I want a box of spare ammo for every man."

Everyone except Cass Benedict started to file out but stopped when Riley pointed at Fargo and said, "What about this jasper, boss? Want me to do him in?"

"No!"

The cry came from Amanda. Her brother and Gheller turned to her in some surprise. Arthur put a hand on her shoulder and said, "Disposing of him is the wise thing to do, sis. He knows too much."

"I agree," Amanda replied, "but I demand the right

to do it myself." She gave Fargo the same hungry look a cat would give a canary. "I offered myself to him and he jilted me. No man has ever done that before. I want to kill him nice and slow. I want to hear him scream as he dies and see the life fade from his eyes."

"It makes no difference to me who does it," Gheller said impatiently, "just so it gets done. There will be plenty of time for you to indulge yourself after we've visited the Mackenzies. He'll keep until then."

"Just be sure to leave someone here to watch him," Arthur suggested.

Gheller opened the door. "Riley, you're elected. As soon as you have the horses set to go, I want—"

"Why me?" the pudgy gunman objected. "I've been with you from the beginning, boss. I have a right to be there when we get what's ours." He gestured at a gunman with a scar on his temple. "Have Harris do it. He won't mind."

"Very well. Harris, as soon as you're done helping Riley, make yourself comfortable until we get back. Don't let anyone in. If our friend tries to escape, shoot him in the knees. He won't try twice."

"Will do, boss."

In a span of seconds Fargo found himself alone with Kenny's corpse. He immediately worked his wrists and ankles back and forth, attempting to wriggle free, but Riley had tied the knots sadistically tight. Wriggling only caused the hemp to bite deeper into his flesh. Regardless, he stuck at it, surging with all his might against his bounds. All he had to do was loosen them a quarter of an inch or so. But it was new rope, with no give, and would take hours. Hours he didn't have. Gripping the chair arms, he began to rock his body from side to side. His goal was to flip the chair over onto its side in the hope it would break when it hit the floor. But hardly had the chair's legs begun to move when a light knock at the door froze him in place.

"Mr. Gheller? Are you in here?" The door opened wide enough for a grizzled specimen in his sixties or seventies to poke his head inside. "It's me. Doc Wilson."

His eyes were horribly bloodshot and he slurred his words. "Cavendish said you wanted to see me."

"Come on in, Doc," Fargo said amiably. "I'm glad to see you."

"Most folks are. Or were, anyway, before I ruined my career with booze." Teetering like a windblown reed, Wilson shuffled in and shut the door behind him. In his left hand was a scuffed black bag. One of its two grips was missing and it had a hole in the side. His clothes were in equally shabby condition. Smacking his chapped lips, he squinted toward the cot. "Is that one I'm supposed to help?"

An idea suddenly occurred to Fargo. A crazy idea, as loco as could be, but given how drunk Wilson was it just might work. "Both of us," he said.

"You, too?" Wilson staggered over. His breath reeked, and he couldn't stand straight if his life depended on it. "What's wrong? You appear hearty and hale to me." He patted Fargo's wrist and his palm scraped the rope. "I say. Why are you tied up? Who are you? What's this all about?"

"I was bit by a wolf."

Doc Wilson's bloodshot eyes narrowed and he looked Fargo up and down. "Where? I don't see any bite marks."

"On my leg two weeks ago. It's healed by now," Fargo said. "Gheller feared the wolf might be rabid so I agreed to be kept in here until we could be sure I wasn't infected." The yarn wasn't as preposterous as it sounded. Rabies was widely feared, and those bitten by suspected carriers were often quarantined.

"Why wasn't I consulted?" Wilson said indignantly. "Rabies are nothing to sneeze at. It's incurable, you know. Once you get it you're done for. The most horrible death conceivable. I saw a fellow die from it once and I couldn't stand to watch." The old man grimaced. "Yet another of the revolting images I'll take with me to my grave. And people wonder why I turned to liquor." He looked around. "Say, Mr. Gheller isn't here, is he?"

"He had to tend to business," Fargo said. "So he asked me to explain."

"Let's get started." Doc Wilson fiddled with the clasp on his black bag and after a minute succeeded in opening it. Fargo thought he was after his medical instruments, but the old man pulled out a silver flask. "I hope you won't mind if I indulge. My nerves aren't as steady as they should be."

"Help yourself," Fargo said. "Just so you give me a clean bill of health. I've been cooped up in here so long I could scream."

"First things first." Wilson tipped the flask to his mouth and greedily gulped. Sighing happily, he replaced the cap, shoved the flask into his bag, and adopted a professional bearing. Or as professional as he could three sheets to the wind. "Now then, you say it's been two weeks since you were bitten?"

"Yes." Fargo winced as Wilson poked his neck and face. The man had the medical finesse of a bull buffalo.

"Hmm. No swelling of the glands, no swelling of the face, either. That's a good sign, young man. A very good sign."

"So you'll cut me loose?" Fargo urged, afraid at any moment Harris would return.

"Be patient, sonny. We can't rush these things. Rabies is highly contagious. The welfare of the community is at stake." Wilson prodded some more. "Let's see. What else am I supposed to check?" he asked himself. "Ah yes. The eyes." Bending, he pressed a finger onto Fargo's right eyelid and held it open so he could examine the pupil. Up close his breath was unbelievably foul, a revolting mix of coffin varnish, vomit, and other unsavory odors.

Fargo came close to gagging. He tried holding his breath, but the stench crept up his nostrils as if it were a living thing.

"Your eyes don't seem dilated. That's another good sign," Doc Wilson said. "Have you had any stiffness in your joints? Any problem with sore muscles?"

"No," Fargo said. Some of the reek washed into his

mouth and down his throat. His stomach churned and he felt his gorge start to rise.

"Excellent." Wilson stepped back, his grizzled chin bobbing. "You'll be glad to hear it's my esteemed opinion you don't have the rabies. Inform Mr. Gheller he can set you free."

"He said you were to do it," Fargo said.

"Me?" Wilson swayed unsteadily, caught himself, then fumbled at the clasp to his bag and rummaged around inside. "I had a scalpel in here somewhere. Last time I used it was on a Swedish fellow, a farmer who was spider-bit. A brown recluse got him in the leg when he was out in his barn, and the venom was eating it away. I had to scrape away a bowlful of rotting flesh to save him."

Fargo stared at the door, at the latch. "Hurry it up, Doc." There was no telling how much longer Harris would be gone. "Cut these ropes."

Wilson felt about in the black bag a while longer. "I'd like to oblige you, son, but I can't find my damn scalpel. I must have pawned it back when I pawned my stethoscope and a lot of other stuff. My memory isn't what it used to be, either."

"I have a knife," Fargo revealed. "It's in a sheath inside my right boot, strapped to my ankle. Use that instead."

"Well, isn't that convenient!" Grinning, Doc Wilson squatted. Or tried to. In his inebriated state his legs gave out and he plopped onto his backside. Cackling merrily, he slapped the floor and exclaimed, "Did you see? Add my knees to that list of things that aren't what they should be."

"Try again," Fargo said. He thought he'd heard footsteps but must have been mistaken because no one came to the door.

Tittering, Doc Wilson placed both hands flat and tried to rise. "Give me a second. Sometimes this takes some doing." His spindly arms were quaking, and after only five or six seconds he gave up and sank back down.

"Whew. That tuckered me out. I think I need another drink."

No! Fargo almost shouted, spurred by growing desperation. "It can wait. Getting me out of this chair is more important."

"Just another few seconds." Wilson snagged hold of the black bag. Clasping the flask to him as if it were a lover, he enjoyed a long swig. "Ahhhh. The elixir of life. If they don't have whiskey in heaven I'll be better off down below."

"How about these ropes?" Fargo reminded him. "You don't need to get up. Just slide over to the chair."

"Why didn't I think of that?" Concentrating, Doc Wilson laboriously pushed himself the three feet separating them. "I did it!" he crowed. "How about that!" He looked from one boot to the other. "Which foot did you say it was again?"

"The right."

Wilson raised his hands, then blinked. "I hate to be the bearer of bad tidings, sonny, but we have a problem."

Fargo leaned forward as far as he could. He hadn't realized it, but the rope was looped around his pant leg near the top of the boot in such a way as to prevent the sawbones from sliding his fingers underneath. "See if you can undo the knots."

"I'll try. But don't expect miracles. My fingers are worse off than my knees." Wilson tugged. He pried. He lowered himself onto all fours and gnawed at the knots with his teeth. "I'm sorry. I just can't do it," he conceded defeat.

There had to be another way, Fargo told himself. Looking right and left, he spied an ax over in the corner opposite the cot. Used for chopping firewood, he figured. "There! Try that!"

Doc Wilson gripped the chair and pulled himself erect. Tottering, he shambled over and attempted to lift the ax but couldn't. "Damn. This thing is heavy." Grunting, he started to slide it across the floor. "I'm not so sure this is a good idea, son."

Neither was Fargo, but he had run out of options. He

heard the drum of hooves fading to the north, then the sound of someone whistling. Whistling that grew steadily louder as the whistler neared the shack.

It had to be Harris. In another few seconds the gun-man would be there.

12

Skye Fargo couldn't wait for Doc Wilson to free him any longer. He had to do it by himself and he had to do it quickly. Levering onto his toes, he heaved upward, raising the heavy chair off the floor. He couldn't rise very high strapped down as he was, but it was enough to permit him to pivot and let gravity take over. Even though he was braced for the crash it still jarred him. A sharp *crack*, and his right elbow spiked with pain. The chair arm had snapped, and the rope binding his wrist went slack. Working swiftly, he tore his right forearm loose and bent down to tear at the loops around his right boot.

The man outside wasn't more than twenty feet from the shack.

Fargo tugged harder, but the knot resisted. Unless he could get his hands on a weapon Harris would foil his escape. Again he glanced around the room, and this time saw a full metallic glimmer under the cot. Kenny's revolver was lying where it had fallen after it slipped from the young gunman's grasp. "Bring me that pistol," he directed the sawbones.

Doc Wilson stopped hauling on the ax. "What good will a gun do? You're not thinking of shooting those ropes off, are you?"

"The gun!" Fargo shouted. In doing so he alerted Harris, because the whistling abruptly stopped.

Startled, Doc Wilson stepped to the cot and doubled over. "No need to snap my head off, son. I might be old, but I'm not deaf. My ears are one of the few parts of me that still works."

Footsteps approached the door. Fargo thought Harris would barge on in, but the gunman wasn't taking undue chances. Fargo's mention of a gun had instilled caution. The latch began to rise, but slowly.

Doc Wilson tottered toward the chair clasping a short-barreled version of the same model Colt Fargo used. "Here you go. But why all the rush? It's not as if you're going anywhere?" He giggled at his joke.

The latch was almost as high as it could go. Harris was seconds from entering.

Wrenching on the chair, Fargo twisted and thrust his hand at Wilson. "The Colt! Now!" Something in his tone made the old man jump to obey. The instant Fargo's palm wrapped around the butt, he swiveled toward the door and thumbed back the hammer.

A heartbeat later the door was flung open and in bounded Harris, his revolver trained on the spot where Fargo would be if the chair were upright. Quick as a cat he perceived the true situation and compensated.

Fargo fired first. Two shots boomed in the shack's confines and Harris was catapulted back out the door to sprawl in the dust.

Doc Wilson was flabbergasted. "I'll be horsewhipped! What did you go and do that for, sonny? Didn't he work for Mr. Gheller?"

"Bring me the ax," Fargo said. When the older man didn't move fast enough to suit him he leveled the Colt as incentive. For all he knew, Gheller had left other gunnies in Lodestone beside Harris and they would rush to the scene.

"Be careful where you're pointing that hogleg!" Doc Wilson bleated. Gripping the ax's long handle in both hands, he bent his frail back to the task.

Fargo was listening for footfalls, but heard shouts instead. From the direction of the saloon came a yell demanding to know what the shooting was about. Someone over near Big Nose Kate's tent answered he had no idea and wasn't about to have his head shot off venturing to find out. Fargo beckoned at Wilson, who had stopped to catch a breath.

"I'm coming, I'm coming," the sawbones groused, and resumed pulling. "I just wish you would tell me what this is all about. I'm not looking to get into trouble with Mr. Gheller. He won't like what you did."

"Leave Gheller to me," Fargo said. His impatience climbing, he crabbed toward his reluctant rescuer, dragging the chair along with him. As soon as the ax was within reach he set the Colt down and seized the handle. Wielding it one-handed took some doing, but by holding it a few inches below the head he could swing it fairly effectively. His initial blow shattered the left chair arm. His next reduced the chair's right leg to splinters. From there it was only a matter of removing the last loops and standing.

"You're mighty spry for a fellow who has been tied down for two weeks," Doc Wilson commented.

Fargo reloaded the Colt with cartridges from his gun belt and shoved the revolver into his holster. It wasn't his, but it would suffice. The Henry had been left propped against the wall, another mistake Gheller and his bunch would regret.

Wilson was fumbling for his flask. "If I had any money I'd go on a bender to end all benders."

Fishing in a pocket, Fargo tossed him five dollars. "That's for helping me. If I don't make it back you'd be wise to make yourself scarce." It was possible Gheller might link the doctor to his escape and take revenge.

Wilson grinned crookedly. "I'll just drink myself into a stupor, crawl under my blankets, and pull them over my head. It's what I've been doing for pretty near thirty years." He swilled more rotgut. "Running wouldn't do me any good, son. In the shape I'm in I wouldn't get very far."

"Does Lodestone have a stable?" Fargo hadn't seen one, but he needed a horse, and needed it right away.

"You're joshing. In a dump this size?" Whiskey trickled over Wilson's lower lip and down his chin. "The closest thing we have is a corral, just past the tents to the northwest. Mr. Gheller owns it. He boards horses in half and reserves the rest for him and his gunnies so they can get to their animals quick-like if they need to. No one is allowed to lay a hand on his stock or there will be—"

Fargo rushed out the door. He had heard all he needed, and he couldn't afford to waste another moment. Gheller's outfit had too much of a head start. To overtake them before they reached the hidden canyon would take some doing, especially without the Ovaro. Other than the usual loud racket emanating from the Aces High, Lodestone lay quiet under the stars. The line in front of Big Nose Kate's had shortened considerably and few other people were abroad. No one tried to stop him as he wound among the tents.

Soon Fargo came to the corral, a crude affair constructed from trimmed saplings. It was divided down the middle, just as Doc Wilson had said. On the right were about a dozen horses, some dozing, some nipping at hay that had been strewn about. In the left half was a solitary sorrel. Gheller's, Fargo suspected as he hurried to a gate. Beside it, draped over the top rail, were a saddle and bridle. Without hesitation Fargo hoisted them onto his shoulder, along with a saddle blanket he found folded underneath, and opened the gate. The sorrel shied but calmed down once he spoke softly and stroked its neck. Within three minutes he was mounted and galloping northward along the stream.

Fargo figured the outlaws had a ten-to-fifteen–minute lead. It sounded like a lot, but he still had a chance to catch up. *If* Arthur and Amanda were late reaching the rendezvous spot, and *if* the siblings and Gheller spent some time discussing how they intended to go about slipping into the canyon and disposing of the Mackenzies, and *if* they took their sweet time getting there, he might overtake them in time to save Bethany and her mother.

Clouds were scuttling across the sky from the west, harbingers of rain by morning. An inky blanket mantled the landscape, working as much in Fargo's favor as against him. The outlaws wouldn't be able to spot him until he was right on top of them. Unfortunately, the reverse was also true, and if he blundered onto them in the dark it could have dire consequences.

As if to prove him right, out of the night materialized several weary prospectors trudging homeward.

Fargo was almost on top of them before he knew it. Hauling on the reins, he brought the sorrel to a stop a few feet from the foremost.

"Damn, mister! You almost trampled me!" the man complained.

"First those other gents, now you," said a second gold-seeker.

"How many were there?" Fargo asked. "And how far behind them am I?"

The three glanced at one another. "Wasn't there eleven?" the foremost prospector said. "Or did I miss a few?"

"No, Fred, there were eleven," confirmed the third man. "I counted them as they went by."

The second prospector scratched his beard. "I'd reckon they're about five minutes ahead of you, mister. Riding hellbent for leather."

"Thanks." Encouraged by the news, Fargo jabbed his spurs against the sorrel. He still had a chance. Once he overtook them, though, then what? Alone, he was no match for eleven cutthroats. Not without an edge. The only thing he could think of was to circle on ahead and reach the giant slabs of rock before they did. The slabs were the only cover along that particular stretch of the stream. Fortified behind them, he could hold off the outlaws indefinitely. Long enough, at any rate, for Bethany and Marjorie to join him, and between the three of them they might be able to drive the pack of killers off.

Fargo rode hard, pushing the sorrel, using the reins and his spurs much more liberally than he was accustomed to. It couldn't be helped. Three lives were at stake, two of them women he liked and admired. He would be damned if he would let the Suttons and Slan Gheller murder them.

The sorrel's flying hooves rang loudly on the small stones covering the ground, raising enough racket to be heard hundreds of yards away. But the outlaws were bound to be raising a racket of their own, a louder racket since there were more of them, and Fargo deemed it unlikely they'd hear him. Not that he would go any slower even if he thought they could.

Negotiating the stream's many serpentine twists and turns was nerve-wracking. Fargo never knew when he would gallop around a bend and spot the gunmen. Each time he came to one, he tensed, ready to pull the Henry from the scabbard, but each time he was disappointed.

The sorrel was doing its best, but it lacked the Ovaro's speed and stamina. The stallion was a superb animal, fleeter than most, with the endurance of a mountain goat, traits that had saved Fargo's hash countless times. By comparison the sorrel was merely average. Fargo realized his hope of overtaking the outlaws had been premature; they would reach the canyon well before him.

Fargo prayed Marjorie and Bethany weren't asleep. That one or the other would hear the gunmen coming, and they would seek cover.

The sorrel sped on, its mane streaming, giving all it had. Seconds were hours. Minutes were eternities. At any moment Fargo might hear the crackle of gunfire. He dreaded arriving at the grotto to find it was all over, dreaded the Mackenzies might be added to the long list of innocent victims the Suttons and Gheller had tallied.

Then Fargo swept around one last bend and up ahead were the gigantic slabs. He saw movement, saw horses, and instantly slowed. Snaking the Henry out, he levered a cartridge into the chamber.

No shots thundered an unwelcome chorus. No yells pealed off the high ramparts. The horses had been left there, and the outlaws had gone on afoot. Drawing rein, Fargo vaulted from the saddle while the sorrel was still in motion. He ran in among the slabs and made straight for the gap. He was through in no time. As he hurtled into the canyon he glimpsed a flickering glow off up the canyon, at the grotto. The Mackenzies were still awake and had a fire going.

Fargo couldn't understand why the canyon was so

quiet, why he hadn't heard gunshots, until he remembered Slan Gheller's fondness for torture. Pouring every ounce of energy he had into his legs, he ran for all he was worth. But he was too late.

The outlaws had taken Marjorie and Bethany by surprise. Mother and daughter were on their knees by the fire, glaring at their captors. Behind them stood the Suttons. In front of Bethany, leering lecherously, was Slan Gheller. Perry Hutchings lay bundled under blankets, unconscious. The rest of the outlaws were scattered about the grotto, some examining the rich veins of ore, others sorting through the pile of saddlebags and pouches. Cass Benedict was by himself, nearer to the opening than anyone else.

Fargo stalked through the trees and hunkered behind an oak. He leveled the Henry but didn't shoot. Not yet. The women might be caught in the crossfire.

Gheller was addressing Bethany. ". . . so high and mighty, are you? All those airs you put on. All those times you snubbed me, treating me like I was dirt. You never imagined your lives would be in my hands, to do with as I please."

"Shoot us and be done with it, you mangy bastard," Marjorie declared. "Or are you fixin' to talk us to death."

"It won't be that easy, old woman," Gheller said. "I want to take my time. I want to hear you beg for mercy."

"That'll be the day," Marjorie responded. "I'd rather eat hog slop than kowtow to the likes of you."

Gheller slapped her, slapped her so hard Marjorie was knocked flat. Bethany reached over to help, crying out, "Ma!" and Gheller savagely shoved her. "Leave her be! The old hag is getting what she deserves. For months I've had to put up with her looking down her nose at me. No more! Now I'm in control. Now I have it all!"

Arthur Sutton interrupted. "*You* have it all, Slan? Aren't you forgetting my sister and me? We're equal partners, remember?"

"Better be careful, Slan," Amanda said. "You wouldn't want us to get the impression you intend to keep all the gold for yourself, now would you?"

"Be serious," Gheller laughed to dismiss the notion, a blatantly insincere laugh, exactly like back at the shack when the Suttons questioned him about the exchange of lead with Cass, Riley, and Kenny. This time, however, the Suttons didn't let it pass without comment. This time Amanda took a couple of steps to the right and rested her hand on her revolver.

"Know what I think, Slan? I think you did send your three boys to kill us. And now you have it in your devious little mind to cheat us and keep the gold for yourself. So I guess it's best if we end our partnership." Amanda paused. "What do you think?"

Slan Gheller went pale, then glanced at his hired guns. They had stopped what they were doing, and were converging. His confidence restored, Gheller repaid Amanda's grin with one of his own. "What if I am planning to keep it all?" he said cockily. "There are nine of us an only two of you. You can't possibly drop us all."

Gheller's gunnies ringed the siblings. Riley and a few others were plainly eager to throw down on them. All Gheller had to do was give the word.

Amanda was unruffled by the turn of events. "No, we couldn't. But we'd sure as hell take half of you with us." Surveying the gunmen, she raised her voice. "There's a better way of settling this, gentlemen. Tell me something. How much gold has your employer promised to give each of you? A thousand dollars' worth? Ten thousand?"

They swapped glances, and Riley answered for the rest, "Mr. Gheller hasn't said yet. But I expect it will be a lot. Ten thousand at least."

"Is that all?" Amanda's contempt was masterly. "Do you call that being generous? I don't. My brother and I would like to offer you ten times as much. A hundred thousand dollars to each and every man."

Astonishment mixed with avarice rippled from face to face. "Did I hear you right?" Riley asked. "A hundred thousand dollars? What do we have to do to earn it?"

Arthur broke his silence. "Switch allegiances. Work for us instead of Gheller. And to demonstrate your new loyalty, kill him where he stands."

Slan Gheller took a step back. "Hold on, now. These men work for me. I never got around to saying what their shares would be because I never knew exactly how much gold was involved."

"Oh please," Arthur said. "Everyone in the valley heard the tales. Everyone knew the mother lode was worth millions. The real reason you never made these fine fellows an offer is because you're too miserly to share your wealth. My sister and I aren't nearly as greedy."

Riley and Dixon and the other outlaws were gazing at Gheller like wolves sizing up a buck they were about to devour. "How about it, boss?" Riley said. "Are you willing to give us as much as they are?"

Fargo expected Gheller to say yes. Any sensible person would. But Slan Gheller's greed got the better of him.

"I can't say yet exactly how much your shares will be. Once I've set up a mining operation and can estimate how much profit there will be over and above the operating expenses, then, and only then, will I be able to assess shares."

Riley slowly nodded. "You and your profit, boss. That's all you really care about, isn't it?" He nodded at the gleaming veins that laced the rear wall. "There's enough gold there to make all of us rich—"

"Millionaires many times over," Arthur interjected.

"Millions," Riley parroted, aglow at the prospect. "But we're not good enough to share with, are we?" It was a statement, not a question.

Fargo saw many of the gunmen go hard around the eyes and mouth, and suspected what would happen next. A notable exception was Cass Benedict, who stayed aloof from the brewing conflict and was staring thoughtfully at Marjorie Mackenzie.

Gheller held his hands out in front of him. "Now you just hold on. All of you. I'm still in charge here. I'm still the man who hired you. What I say goes."

"Not anymore," Riley said, and drew his pistol. A majority of the rest did the same. Gun hammers clicked like crickets as gun muzzles were trained on the man the guns were supposed to protect.

"Have you taken leave of your senses!" Slan Gheller blustered. "Holster your hardware this instant and I'll be willing to forget this whole incident."

"That's damned decent of you," Riley said, and squeezed the trigger.

More revolvers boomed, blast after blast, loud as thunder. At each retort Slan Gheller was punched backward. At each shot another hole blossomed in his ravaged torso. Blood spouted like a geyser, spraying over the floor, over the fire, the flames consuming it with a loud hiss. Slan Gheller melted into a broken heap, convulsed violently a few times, and breathed his last.

"And that's that," Amanda said. Walking over, she nudged the body with the tip of a black boot. "As easy as taking candy from a baby."

"All that's left is to dispose of the Mackenzies and the claim is ours," Arthur said. He moved around in front of them. "Which of you ladies wants to die first?"

Fargo wedged the Henry to his shoulder. He would do what he could to save the women, even at the cost of his own life. But as he sighted on Arthur, someone else came to their defense.

"No one is harming a hair on their heads," Cass Benedict declared, his hands loose at his side, his right palm brushing the ivory handle of his Colt.

The other gunmen were too cowed by his reputation to dispute him. Not Amanda Sutton. Arching an eyebrow, she taunted, "I beg your pardon?"

"You heard me," the small gunman said. "The ladies and I are leaving. Anyone who tries to stop us answers to me."

Arthur Sutton smirked. "Why, I do believe that was a threat. Am I to take it you have no interest in working for us, Mr. Benedict?"

"I was hired by Slan Gheller. With him gone I'm free to do as I please. And I don't abide hurting women."

"Well now," Arthur said, "that puts us at an impasse.

Because the only way you're taking them out of here is over our dead bodies."

Amanda was a coiled rattlesnake primed to strike. "In case you can't count, little man, there are a lot more of us than there are of you. You can't kill ten people with six shots."

Fargo strode from concealment. "How about twelve shots?" he said, covering the outlaws with his Henry as he moved to Cass Benedict's side.

For once Arthur and Amanda were speechless with surprise. Amanda, predictably, recovered first and pointed at the rifle. "You'll only get one or two of us with that. Then the rest will turn you into a sieve."

"Guess who I'll shoot first?" Fargo gave her something to ponder. To Bethany and Marjorie he said, "Get up and get out. Take Hutchings with you. Quickly."

Marjorie started to object, but Bethany gripped her by the shoulders and forcibly hustled her to the detective, who opened his eyes and mumbled incoherently as the two women propped his limp form between them and hastened toward the entrance.

None of the gunmen tried to interfere.

Fargo shoved the Henry into Bethany's hand as they passed him. As soon as the women were swallowed by the night, he glanced at Cass Benedict. "Want to give the damn gazettes something to write about?"

The small gunman smiled. "You start on the left, I'll start on the right, and we'll work toward the center."

Fargo preferred to start in the middle with the Suttons. Amanda was uncommonly fast, and while he hadn't seen her brother draw, something told him Arthur was just as fast, if not faster.

Suddenly Amanda stabbed for her revolver, screeching like a banshee, "Kill them! Kill the sons of bitches!"

Fargo's hand streaked down and out. To his right there was a flash of ivory, a fraction before his pistol was clear, and Cass Benedict's Colt banged a fraction before his. Benedict's slug took down a gunman on the far right. His first shot slammed into Amanda, smashing her back with her arms windmilling. His second caught Arthur in the shoulder and spun the brother around. His third exploded Dixon's cheek in a fountain of gore. Several other outlaws were already down, thanks to Benedict.

Riley was on one knee, scarlet pouring from a rib wound, trying to steady his gun hand with the other. Thumbing back the hammer, Fargo cored Riley's forehead.

Amanda screeched again and staggered toward them, firing with each step. Her veil had been dislodged and her once lovely features were contorted in pure hatred.

Fargo felt a stinging sensation in his left shoulder, another in his right leg. He heard repeated thuds as leaden hail struck Cass Benedict, but the small gunman never stopped firing. Cass's next shot added a new hole between Amanda's eyes, the impact flipping her off her feet. Arthur had switched his pistol from one hand to the other and was about to shoot. Fargo sent a bullet into him. Cass Benedict sent a bullet into him. Arthur still wouldn't fall.

Taking deliberate aim, Fargo expended his last cartridge and blew off the top of Arthur Sutton's head.

Two more shots sounded, shots fired from out of the dark. Bethany Mackenzie appeared, wisps of gunsmoke rising from the Henry.

The outlaws were all on the ground, several twitching in their death throes.

Fargo looked down at himself, at a rip in his shirt and blood on his leg. Neither were serious. He turned, and barely thrust out his arms in time to catch Cass Benedict as the small gunman pitched forward. "Cass?"

Benedict's gray eyes focused on his. "Did we do it? Are the women safe?"

"They're safe," Fargo said, his throat muscles tightening.

"I have a sister in Des Moines. Susan Benedict. See to it she gets the money in my saddlebags. It's not much, only two hundred and twenty dollars, but she has four kids to feed."

"Consider it done."

Cass's hand groped for Fargo's, and squeezed. "I'm obliged," he said quietly. The next moment he was gone.

Fargo became aware of Bethany standing at his shoulder. He had to cough before he could get his vocal chords to work. "Bring me a shovel. I'll bury him myself, now."

"Are you sure?" Bethany said. "You've been hit. I'll go to the spring for water and bandage you up."

"Later," Fargo insisted, lifting the fallen gunman. "Fetch your mother and Hutchings. After I'm done I'll go into Lodestone for Doc Wilson, sober him up, and bring him out to do what he can."

"There's no hurry," Bethany said. "Mr. Hutchings isn't that bad off. Give him a month and he'll be good as new. Everyone else is dead." She gazed quizzically at Cass Benedict. "Why did he help us like that? Was he a good man at heart?"

"One of the best," Skye Fargo said.

LOOKING FORWARD!

The following is the opening section from the next novel in the exciting *Trailsman* series from Signet:

THE TRAILSMAN #238

CHEROKEE JUSTICE

Indian Territory, 1859—
There is no Sunday west of St. Louis—
no God west of Fort Smith.

Skye Fargo rode slowly on his Ovaro, entering Fort Smith, Arkansas from the north. The road was dusty and the day muggy. Clouds building in the south promised rain to take the edge off the stifling summer heat, but Fargo knew better than to count on a downpour. This time of year Arkansas was well known for its changeable, erratic weather.

But the weather was nowhere near as unpredictable as his old buddy Coot Marlowe. Fargo had been trading hard-won buffalo hides for not enough money up in St. Louis when he had received the telegram urging him to come visit for a spell. Coot had a knack for finding men and had unerringly located him almost a year after they parted ways up in the Dakotas. Fargo had been sorry to see Coot go, especially to become a bounty hunter. While tracking down owlhoots might be a job that needed doing, Fargo thought Coot could better use his skills out in the Rockies or up in the Bitterroots.

Still, Arkansas was a green, lush place and seemed hospitable enough. And wherever Coot was, there were always plenty of wide eyed does willing to curl up with him in his bedroll.

Fargo wiped the sweat from his face with his faded blue bandanna and then held a hand up to shade his eyes. As he rode, he noted the deserted streets, empty houses, and vacant stores. It was as if Fort Smith had been driven off by some unknown threat. Fargo wondered if that might be possible until he heard the distant buzz of a large crowd toward the center of town. He turned his Ovaro and saw more and more people hurrying in the same direction, like ants invading a spill of sugar on a kitchen table.

"What's the big ruckus?" Fargo called to a bespectacled man locking his bookstore before joining the trail of men and women.

"You just ride in, mistuh?"

"I did, sir," Fargo said.

"They're going to hang that son of a bitch. Nobody wants to miss that!" Without further explanation, the man hurried off, his short legs pumping hard to keep him moving at the same speed as the others around him.

Fargo had seen his fill of executions, but the chance that Coot was there too, kept Fargo moving in the direction of the Fort Smith town square. The large open area held a gazebo. Next to it a large gallows loomed like a wooden vulture waiting for something to die. Men milled around the gallows doing this and that, but most focused their attention on the half dozen well-dressed men in the gazebo.

Fargo heaved a sigh. He recognized the politicians immediately. They took every chance they could get to make a speech, no matter that desperados were going to get their necks stretched for crimes so horrible women fainted and strong men blanched.

"There you are," came a familiar voice. "Figured you'd be here in time to see the fireworks."

"They shoot off firecrackers at executions in Forth Smith?" Fargo asked. He dismounted and went to his old friend. Coot Marlowe about crushed him with a bear hug, and Fargo returned it. They slapped each another on the back and then pushed apart.

"You're a sight for sore eyes, Fargo. You ain't changed a bit, 'cept you don't smell like a buffalo anymore. What happened? You run into a rain shower on the road?" Coot was a huge man with an even bigger appetite. Fargo had missed him sorely.

"No rain," Fargo said, knowing he was being joshed. "I hitched my wagon to a couple of those big catfish out in the Mississippi and let them pull me along so I'd arrive all fresh and rested."

The trail dust and the lather on the Ovaro's sides put this to the lie, but the two had always swapped tall tales. Fargo remembered fondly when Coot had once told him how he had a mule that died during an especially hot summer in Nebraska. The corn in the field had popped from the heat, leaving a white blanket close to two feet deep as far as the eye could see. The mule saw this, and not being too bright, thought it was snow and froze to death on the spot. It had taken Fargo a week to come up with a topper.

"Come on around here so we can get a good look at the festivities," Coot said, guiding Fargo through the fringe of the crowd and down a side street. They weaved in and out of narrow alleys and back streets until emerging again not fifty feet from the gallows.

"You have something to do with the men who're going to hang?" Fargo asked.

"Funny that you should say that," Coot said, grinning crookedly. "As a matter of pure fact, I was the one who tracked 'im down and brought 'im back to Judge Ringo."

"Judge Ringo's the presiding judge in these parts?"

"A fair man, but over his head when it gets down to enforcin' the laws. He has political aspirations reachin' far from these fine rollin' hills, with an outlaw lurkin' behind every one."

"Heard tell the lawless element is running wild here," Fargo said. "Why's that when a man like you is here to chase them down?"

"Injun country, that's why," Coot said, turning sober. "They head into Indian Territory knowing that the United States Army can't go after them."

Fargo sucked in his breath. He had the feeling Coot's telegram had meant more than wanting to get together for another bender and to reminisce about old times.

"I'm not a bounty hunter,' Fargo said. "Let the law go after criminals. I'm content to—"

"There." Coot said, grabbing his friend's arm with an iron grip. "See that one with the smirk on his face. He still don't believe he's gonna die."

"What'd he do?"

"That's Jason Strain, 'bout the most vicious killer I ever saw. First he killed a man, then his two sons and then raped the woman 'fore killing her too. And that was only for practice. When he was plyin' his trade, he was even meaner."

For a moment Fargo thought Coot might be exaggerating, but the solemn note in his voice spoke the truth as he saw it, with no embellishment.

"Even worse, he's got himself a gang to run with. They do their dirty work over here in Arkansas and then hightail it into Indian Territory where there's not much law."

"What about the cavalry at Fort Gibson?"

Coot snorted in disdain.

"They couldn't find their own asses if they used both hands and had a first class scout helpin' them. Oh, they send out patrols and fight sorties, but mostly they try to keep the Five Civilized Tribes safe from the wild Indians on the western frontiers."

"The Osage?"

"They kick up a fuss," Coot agreed. "So do the Arapahos and the Comanches. The calvary boys don't have much time to track down killers and thieves from outside Indian Territory."

"You want me to partner with you to get the rest of Strain's gang?"

"Hell, Fargo, he ain't even the leader. I can't even call him the worst. I know what you think about bein' a bounty hunter, but look at it more as doin' a public service."

"One that pays well?" Fargo couldn't keep a small smile from creeping to his lips. Coot always had an eye out for the ladies—and a quick buck.

"This one I'd do for nothin'," Coot Marlowe said, and Fargo believed him. Coot looked Fargo square in the eye and said, "I found those dead settlers and saw what Strain'd done. After I brought him in, the rest of the gang went wild and burned out close to twenty other settlers."

Fargo saw that Coot blamed himself for the arson spree.

"That wasn't your fault," Fargo pointed out.

"Not catchin' them was. They're good, Fargo, better 'n me."

Fargo stared silently at his friend. Coot had always considered himself the best there was at whatever he did. Knowing that this bear of a man admitted to being second to a gang of killers was enough to send a shiver down Fargo's spine.

"They're not better'n the Trailsman," Coot finished. "Money doesn't mean that much to you, Fargo. I know that. But I swear on my mama's grave, every dime of reward money we might get is yours. I'll do this for nuthin' but the pleasure of seein' them varmints strung up."

Fargo nodded, then said, "You never had a mama. You crawled out from under a wet rock."

The crack was enough to break Coot's somber mood, as he broke out laughing. "I knew I could count on you, Fargo. Now why don't we watch the law take care of that vermin."

Fargo saw that the politicians had stopped their speech making but refused to give up the moment. They moved to the edge of the crowd, shaking hands and howdying with the men standing up close. Fargo's eyes drifted from the crowd to the gallows—and lower.

He frowned, trying to understand what wasn't right. Men milled around like bees swarming on a brightly colored flower.

"You know them?" he asked Coot.

"The deputies? Most of 'em. Judge Ringo doesn't do too good a job hirin' the best, but then the pay's pretty bad."

"They're practically tripping over each other," Fargo said. "That's a lot of law for just one hanging."

"I told you Strain was a mean son of a bitch," Coot answered, his voice raised so Fargo could hear him over everyone else.

The level of excitement among the Forth Smith masses rose to a pitch until the air was charged, like before a summer storm. "That's Judge Ringo," Coot said. He pointed out a smallish man with a big handlebar mustache and a towering black stovepipe hat, preparing himself to address the crowd. The judge wore a plain broadcloth coat and maintained the appearance of a hellfire-and-brimstone preacher ready to unload a sermon.

In spite of his diminutive size, the judge's voice boomed like thunder as it broke over the crowd. A hush fell as everyone succumbed to the man's spell. Coot had said Judge Ringo had political aspirations and Fargo could believe it. The man had a way of holding the crowd's attention, even if he was only relating what they all knew.

"I have seen some mighty heinous crimes in my day,"

Judge Ringo began, "but those committed by Jason Strain are by far the most reprehensible. I take no pleasure in witnessing his execution, because it does not bring back the men and women that he has wronged so grievously. To ask for God's mercy on such a malignant soul would be an outrage upon the almighty." His voice cracked and roared like thunder as he turned to the condemned man and shot him a scornful look. "Jason Strain," the judge bellowed, clearly playing to the keyed up mob. "As the swing of the trap door begins your downward path to hell, all I have left to say to you is good riddance!"

A cheer went up as a curiously calm Jason Strain mounted the gallows steps. He went to the center of the gallows and stood on the trapdoor as easily as if he went waltzing out in a barn dance.

"Something's wrong," Fargo said. He felt it in his gut even though he was uncertain how to respond to it.

"Nothing can go wrong, they bought new rope just for this execution," Coot told him. "Hell, I would have loaned them my own if they'd needed it."

The execution proceeded. He pulled a black hood over an unresisting Jason Strain's head, and moved the condemned into position. A noose was placed over Strain's head and just as he was about to tighten it everything went to hell.

"There!" shouted Fargo, pushing forward. A spark caught his eye as one of the deputies struck a lucifer and applied to a short length of black miner's fuse. Immediately he went for his Colt as the fuse sputtered and sizzled its way toward a large mound draped in cloth.

Fargo shouted a warning and Coot joined in, but they were too late. . . .